camp CONFIDENTIAL

Suddenly Last Summer

GROSSET & DUNLAP
Published by the Penguin Group
Penguin Group (USA) Inc., 375 Hudson Street,
New York, New York 10014, USA
Penguin Group (Canada), 90 Eglinton Avenue East, Suite 700,
Toronto, Ontario M4P 2Y3, Canada
(a division of Pearson Penguin Canada Inc.)
Penguin Books Ltd., 80 Strand, London WC2R 0RL, England
Penguin Group Ireland, 25 St. Stephen's Green, Dublin 2, Ireland
(a division of Penguin Books Ltd.)
Penguin Group (Australia), 250 Camberwell Road,
Camberwell, Victoria 3124, Australia
(a division of Pearson Australia Group Pty. Ltd.)
Penguin Books India Pvt. Ltd., 11 Community Centre, Panchsheel Park,
New Delhi—110 017, India
Penguin Group (NZ), 67 Apollo Drive, Rosedale,
North Shore 0632, New Zealand
(a division of Pearson New Zealand Ltd.)
Penguin Books (South Africa) (Pty.) Ltd., 24 Sturdee Avenue,
Rosebank, Johannesburg 2196, South Africa

Penguin Books Ltd., Registered Offices:
80 Strand, London WC2R 0RL, England

Cover designed by Ching N. Chan.
Front cover image © Image Source Photography/Endless Summer/Veer Incorporated. Cover background image copyright © Mayang Murni Admin, 2001–2006, www.mayang.com/textures. Text copyright © 2008 by Grosset & Dunlap. All rights reserved. Published by Grosset & Dunlap, a division of Penguin Young Readers Group, 345 Hudson Street, New York, New York 10014. GROSSET & DUNLAP is a trademark of Penguin Group (USA) Inc. Printed in the U.S.A.

Library of Congress Control Number: 2007051759

ISBN 978-0-448-44881-7   10 9 8 7 6 5 4

camp CONFIDENTIAL

Suddenly Last Summer

by Melissa J. Morgan

Grosset & Dunlap

Hey, Tori—

Okay, we both know that for a while you've been trying to convince me of the Wonders of Camp. And I know, I haven't exactly been into it. Because honestly, I would rather be home getting ready for my next competition than sleeping in a wooden shack with a million bugs and no modern plumbing. (I know, I know—you have plumbing.)

But then I got invited to participate in an exhibition at this water sports camp. And it seemed really awesome.

It's called Camp Ohana and it's totally amazing. It's on a beautiful private beach with perfect surfing conditions. After the demonstration, they took us to Turtle Beach, which is this amazing beach where endangered sea turtles come up onto the sand to bask in the sun. With the sunset colors in the sky, I can't tell you how amazing it was.

So: I know you're totally into your bug camp and whatever, but . . . you should think about going to Camp Ohana next year! Then at least we'll both be in Hawaii and I can go visit you and maybe you can come stay with me for a week after camp is over.

I know, I know—you're not as into water sports as I am, but Tor, they teach you anything and everything you'd wanna know. And it's so beautiful there. The beaches in Hawaii are some of the most gorgeous beaches in the world. And think of what it'll do for your tan—not to mention the insta-highlights you'll get just from being out in that sun. I really, really think you would love it! And I know, you really love your friends at Camp Itchy Bunk or whatever, but we're teenagers now—maybe it's time to try something new?

Think about it, okay, Tor?

Love ya,

Cassie

"YIIIIIIIIIIIKES!"

Tori flinched at Jenna's scream as she quickly yanked the wax strip away from her friend's eyebrow.

"*Nice*," Tori announced with a smile, holding up the wax strip for everyone to see. "It's just like my dad said. Kylie Duchamp is the hottest brow specialist in Hollywood, and this kit will make us look like we all had personal sessions with her!"

Jenna wasn't listening—she was too busy wiping tears from her eye. "Holy crap," she murmured. "Who knew that ripping your eyebrow hair out by the root would really *feel* like ripping your hair out by the root?"

Natalie smiled, looking up from the box she'd

been reading. "We have to suffer for beauty, Jenna," she said, moving Jenna's hand to get a better look at her eyebrow. "And I hate to tell you this, but you're not even half done."

Alex, who'd been watching the whole show from her bunk with a nervous expression, stood up. "All right, I'm out," she announced, shaking her head. "Much as I want to be beautiful, I just don't think I can do that."

Tori shrugged, carefully placing another strip below Jenna's eyebrow. "Suit yourself." Without warning, not wanting Jenna to flinch, she grabbed the new strip and ripped it off.

"AAAAUUGH!"

Tori smiled, noting the new shape of Jenna's brow. "Perfect." She glanced over at Alex. "Hey, Al, if you're not going to want your brows done, why don't you make yourself useful and put on a CD from my dad's care package?"

Alex walked over to the box Tori received that day and pushed aside the notes and chichi toiletries. "Which one?"

"Any of them." Tori shrugged. "Oh, you know what? Actually, one of the CDs he sent is from a band where one of the members went to Camp Lakeview when he was a kid. Can you believe that? It just came up in conversation one day."

Alex looked over the CDs. "Wow," she said. "That's such a crazy coincidence. We should definitely give them a shot, then! What are they called?"

Tori struggled to remember for a second, then

it came to her. "Judy Renaissance."

Alex pulled out the CD, unwrapped it, and stuck it in Tori's CD player. She pressed play, and a loud, frantic beat filled the bunk, followed by dueling guitars, and finally layered over with lyrics about staying out all night. Tori liked the song right away—it was bouncy enough to make her want to dance.

"Nice," Alyssa said with a smile, and Tori nodded.

Alex paused by the care package again. "Hey, what's this?" she asked, picking up a computer printout.

"That's my school schedule for next year," Tori replied, placing the third strip on Jenna's other eyebrow.

"Oh my god, can you believe we'll be back in school in three weeks?" Priya asked.

"AAAAUGHH!" screamed Jenna.

"My thought exactly," Priya agreed.

"Can you believe we're going into ninth grade?" Brynn asked, shaking her head. "I can't believe we're almost high schoolers."

Val shook her head. "We're getting old, huh?"

Everyone laughed. Jenna screamed one last time as Tori pulled the last wax strip off. Then everyone gathered around to check out Jenna's new pair of eyebrows—which really *did* look pretty amazing.

"Oh my god, your whole face looks different!" Gaby cried. "It's like you had plastic surgery or something."

Jenna frowned. "Um, where's a mirror?"

Chelsea quickly ran into the bathroom and came back with a little handheld mirror. "Here," she said, handing it to Jenna. "They really do look awesome. Me next!"

Jenna examined her brows in the mirror, turning left and right to see them from different angles. A slow smile spread over her face. "Wow," she murmured. "My eyes look huge. Okay, maybe that was *almost* worth the pain."

Tori laughed. "You look great, Jenna," she said, pulling a section of Jenna's layered brown hair out of her eyes and grabbing a bobby pin to pin it to the crown of her head. "Look at that! You look so much older and more polished."

Jenna tilted her head in the mirror, still smiling. "Wait till David sees," she said softly.

"How are you and David with the long-distance thing?" Nat piped up, looking curious. "I mean, it can be tough sometimes, but you two always seem pretty in sync."

Jenna nodded. "You know, we just talk a lot on the phone and try to see each other as much as we can." She stood up, biting her lip. "I miss him when he's not around. But we always know we'll get the whole summer together at camp."

Nat nodded slowly, considering this. Tori watched her friend with curiosity. Nat had just reunited with her boyfriend of last summer, Logan—someone she'd broken up with last year because the distance thing was too hard. Was she already wondering whether they should break up again this year?

Tori's mind wandered as Chelsea sat down in front of her. She used the stencil from the kit to draw Chelsea's perfect brow shape with a white eyeliner pencil. *Next summer.* It seemed a world away, but she knew it wasn't. There were only two weeks left of camp, then school would start up, then time would fly, and before they knew it, it would be June again. Tori tried to picture a summer *without* Camp Lakeview—like, if she took her cousin Cassie up on her offer to check out Camp Ohana. Tori had to admit that it sounded pretty sweet. But the thought of not seeing her camp friends again formed a little knot of worry in the pit of Tori's stomach.

But maybe that's a good thing, Tori told herself, placing the wax strip on Chelsea's brow. *Maybe that's growing up.*

"YIIIIIKES!" cried Chelsea, grabbing at her brow as Tori yanked the strip off. "Do you have to do it that fast?"

"Would you rather I drew it out so you could feel every little hair pulling out?" Tori asked.

Chelsea sighed. "Ow. Whatever. Let's just get this over with so I can be gorgeous."

Tori tried to hide her smile. Chelsea had grown on her during her three summers of camp. All the girls had, especially Nat, who was Tori's best friend now. Most of them had been coming to Camp Lakeview for four years, and they'd grown up a lot in that time. They'd gone from flirting and crushing on boys to having relationships that spanned years, and they'd gone from sniping and keeping secrets from one another to being the closest friends Tori had ever had.

But they were getting older. Each year, fewer kids their age came back to Camp Lakeview. And watching the younger kids joke around and pull all the same stunts they had pulled in previous summers, Tori had to wonder sometimes if they were too old for Camp Lakeview—were they just coming back because they couldn't let go?

After Tori finished Chelsea's brows, the dinner bell rang.

"Awwww!" cried Priya. "I wanted *my* brows done!"

"Me too!" cried Val.

"Me three!" agreed Candace.

"We can do it later tonight or tomorrow," Tori offered, packing up the kit. "We'll get through everybody, don't worry."

Placing all the pieces back in the pink satin box they'd come in, Tori walked the box over to her cubby and stuck it back in the care package. Her fingers lingered over the package for a second, and when nobody was looking, she grabbed Cassie's letter and shoved it in her pocket.

It couldn't hurt to just bring it up to Nat, she figured.

🏕 🏕 🏕

"Hey." As they walked to the dining hall, Tori grabbed Nat's arm and gently pulled her to the side.

"Hey," Nat replied, looking surprised and distracted. "What's up? When are you going to do *my* eyebrows?"

Tori grinned. "Your eyebrows are already *done*, Nat."

Nat shook her head. "Hello? It's been almost two months since they were touched up." She fingered the spot between her brows with a frown. "I probably look like Albert Einstein already," she murmured.

Tori laughed. "Fine, I'll touch them up tomorrow," she offered. "Look, I wanted—" She paused, looking over at the other girls. They were walking ahead, totally engrossed in their own conversation. Tori lowered her voice, anyway. "There's something I wanted to run by you," she said. "An idea, maybe for next summer."

Nat looked surprised. "You want to be CITs?"

Tori shook her head. "Actually, I was thinking about life *beyond* Camp Lakeview."

Nat frowned. "What do you mean?" she asked.

Feeling weirdly nervous, Tori pulled the letter from her cousin Cassie out of the pocket of her Bermuda shorts. "I mean, Hawaii," she replied. "I mean, surfing and turtles and cute boys . . ."

Nat's frown grew. "*What?*"

Tori paused and sighed. "Look at this," she insisted, pressing Cassie's letter into Nat's hand. "My cousin Cassie visited a surf camp this summer, and it sounds *amazing*. I think we should give it a shot next summer. I mean, we can do some more research, but—"

"You would leave Camp Lakeview?" Nat asked incredulously, looking up from Cassie's letter.

Tori was quiet for a few seconds, surprised. She wasn't one hundred percent convinced that not coming back next year was the right thing to do, either, but there was a weird accusatory tone to Nat's question that she didn't like. "I might," she said. "Is that okay with you?"

Nat's eyes scanned the letter. "I don't even surf, Tori."

Tori was beginning to feel frustrated. "You don't have to—they take beginners," she pointed out. "Nat, have you ever been to Hawaii? It's *incredible*, and that alone is enough to make this camp sound amazing to me. When you add in the surfing, the cute boys—really, how could you say no?"

Nat frowned, still staring at the letter. "I just don't know, Tori," she said. "I mean, yeah, it sounds kind of fun. But Camp Lakeview is a tradition. These girls are my best friends. I don't think—" She sighed. "I don't think I would want to miss out on next summer."

Tori frowned. "Nat, we're all getting older," she said bluntly. "I love everyone, too, but you heard us in there—we're going to be freshmen next year. Everything's changing. Things change. Sooner or later we're going to outgrow Camp Lakeview." She took Cassie's letter back, tucking it into her pocket. "And I know where *I* want to be when that happens."

Nat looked at Tori, surprised. "I can't believe you're so *whatever* about this."

Tori frowned back, feeling a crease form between her eyebrows. "I'm not *whatever*. I'm just telling you how it is."

Nat sighed. "Fine, then. I'll think about it."

Without waiting for Tori's response, Nat turned

around and started running to catch up with the other girls.

▲ ▲ ▲

"So then I was, like, I dunno," Priya was saying later at dinner, telling a story about a boy she was talking to at free swim, "you're clearly nuts, but are you, like, too nuts to take to the social?"

Tori laughed along with the other girls. She still wasn't sure what to make of her tense conversation with Nat, but Priya was pretty funny.

"Priya," Gaby said, "he brought a *swim cap* to camp. A *swim cap*. A swim cap is a deal breaker!"

Priya shrugged sheepishly. "He had the prettiest eyes, though," she said, pausing to take a sip of bug juice. "And I thought maybe he just has really high-maintenance hair?"

Everyone laughed again, and Tori joined in, but a little part of her brain was still preoccupied with what Nat had said.

I can't believe you're so whatever *about this.*

What was she trying to say? That she cared more about their Camp Lakeview friends than Tori did?

It's not like I'd just take off without saying good-bye, Tori thought. *I'd stay in touch with everyone.* She tried to imagine how she would feel next summer, knowing that everyone else had come back to camp and she had gone somewhere else. Would she feel weird, knowing that they were doing all the old traditions without her? *Maybe.* But maybe the new traditions she learned at Camp Ohana would make up for it.

Plus, *boys*. Cute surfer boys. *Nat doesn't know what they're like, living in New York,* Tori thought. *But I, on the other hand . . .* Tori could definitely appreciate the appeal of a cute, toned surfer.

"Tori?" Tori suddenly shook back to life and realized that Chelsea was trying to get her attention.

"Yeah?" Tori asked.

"As I was *saying*, are you bringing a date to the social?"

Tori frowned. "No," she said. She wasn't seeing anyone at camp. Besides, she always had more fun being free to dance with whomever she wanted.

Chelsea turned to Nat. "How about you, Nat?"

Nat glanced up. Actually, she had kind of a faraway look, too—like she was hashing something out in her mind. *Maybe trying to think of a way to apologize to me,* Tori thought cheerfully. *I'm sure she didn't mean to make me look like the bad guy back there.* "What?" Nat asked.

Chelsea sighed. "What is with everybody spacing out tonight?" she asked. "I said, are you taking Logan to the social?"

Nat nodded quickly. "Of course."

"Oh." Chelsea shrugged, taking a sip of bug juice. "I was just wondering, since you guys aren't officially boyfriend and girlfriend and all."

A flash of irritation passed over Nat's eyes, but Tori was pretty sure she was the only one who caught it. Nat and Logan were supposed to be taking it slow—"testing the waters" was the term Tori thought they had used. Lately, though, Nat sure had been spending a lot of time with Logan.

"That doesn't matter," Nat said shortly. "We still really like each other. Of course he'll be my date."

Chelsea nodded. "I just wondered, since you're probably breaking up at the end of the summer, after last year."

Nat's eyes were blazing—like Chelsea had just suggested she cut off her own arm and eat it for dessert.

"Um, that is not a definite," Nat said.

"Have you talked about—"

"Excuse me." Chelsea's next question was cut off by Dr. Steve's voice as he strode up to the microphone. Everyone turned around to look at him. What was up?

"I have an announcement to make," Dr. Steve continued. Actually, now that Tori had a good look at him, she realized that he looked kind of upset. Or nervous or something. He kept fiddling with his sleeve, not quite making eye contact with any of the campers. "We'll have an emergency assembly right after dinner, here in the cafeteria. All campers, counselors, and CITs will attend." He paused. "Thank you." With that, he moved away from the microphone, still not meeting anyone's eyes.

"Whoa," breathed Jenna.

"Whoa is right," Brynn agreed. "What do you think we're in trouble for now?"

Everyone piped up with an idea, talking over one another in their excitement.

"Maybe someone stole something? Something important. Something of Dr. Steve's!"

"Maybe a prank war got out of control."

"Maybe we're being too *cliquey* again," Alex suggested with a roll of her eyes.

"Maybe it's a *good* thing," Val spoke up, a smile spreading over her face. "A field trip! Or a concert! Or the camp is getting a new swimming pool or something!"

Sloan glanced over at Becky and Dahlia, their counselor and CIT. "Do you guys know?"

Becky shook her head. "Nope."

Gaby smiled. "If you did, would you tell us?"

Becky shook her head again. "Nope." She took a sip of water. "But seriously, I don't know. We just heard there would be an assembly tonight after dinner."

As dinner wound to a close, the girls kept piping up with new, increasingly out-there ideas of what the assembly could be for.

"Maybe Camp Lakeview is going to start allowing pets!"

"Maybe we're going on a field trip to New York!"

"Maybe someone flooded the lake with purple dye and now they're in *huge* trouble!"

"Jenna." Becky glanced over at her most prank-loving camper, trying to look concerned. "Is there something I should know about?"

Jenna rolled her eyes. "It's just an *idea*." She paused and in a quieter voice added, "Though it *would* be cool."

Tori was having so much fun listening to her friends' ideas and coming up with more of her own, she almost forgot about the weird convo with Nat and the funny feeling it gave her in the pit of her stomach. *Almost.* Until Nat took a last sip of bug juice, wiped her lips, and looked over at Becky. "Okay if I go sit with Logan's bunk for a minute?"

Tori was usually happy for her friends' romantic success, but something about Nat constantly seeking out Logan worked her last nerve. Maybe it had something to do with Nat getting so uppity with her for wanting to spend a summer away from their friends when Nat was ditching them all the time to hang with Logan. "Have fun," she told her friend sarcastically as Becky nodded and Nat went to take off. "Don't *miss* us too much during the assembly."

Nat glanced back at Tori, a question in her eyes. But Tori just looked away.

A few minutes later, the dull roar of conversations died down as people spotted Dr. Steve walking up to the microphone again. By the time he reached it, the whole dining hall was nearly silent. Clearly 6B wasn't the only bunk dying to find out what was so important that they needed an all-camp assembly.

"Friends," Dr. Steve began, "Camp Lakeview has been open for ninety-two years. In that time generations of campers have come and gone through our gates, enjoying our beautiful grounds, our dedicated staff, and, most importantly, the lifelong friendships that Camp Lakeview creates."

Tori glanced around at her bunkmates. *Lifelong.* See? She could miss one summer and not mess anything up—she knew she would keep in touch with these girls her whole life.

"I have some news." Dr. Steve's voice stumbled, and he paused. "It's difficult to share with you."

Tori felt all of her fellow campers leaning in, feeling concerned. Dr. Steve never got emotional like this. Was there something wrong with Dr. Steve? Was he or someone in his family sick?

Dr. Steve looked around the room, then leaned back into the microphone, speaking quickly. "After ninety-two years, Camp Lakeview will close its doors in two weeks. Camp Lakeview has to close, kids. I'm sorry to tell you that this will be the last summer."

Tori felt her mouth drop open. *I must have heard that wrong*, she thought. But then she turned back to the table and faced all of her friends, all with the same expression she had.

"Camp Lakeview is closing?" hissed Brynn. She looked heartbroken—not the heartbroken look she often wore when she was acting, but a real, stunned, helpless look of horror.

"Camp Lakeview is closing," Dr. Steve repeated, looking around at a sea of stunned faces. "I'm so sorry, kids."

chapter TWO

Nat felt like her heart had exploded. *Closing?* she thought. *Closing for good? That's impossible!*

She looked at Logan, hoping to meet his eye and see that he was as upset about all this as she was. But he was still turned away, waiting for Dr. Steve to go on.

The dining hall was buzzing now. Now that the initial shock had worn off, the campers were all turning to one another, expressing their dismay, throwing out their theories for what went wrong. After a few seconds of this, Dr. Steve tapped on the mike.

"Kids," he said. "Guys. Campers. Let me explain."

The noise died down almost instantly.

Dr. Steve sighed. "As anyone who's come to Camp Lakeview for several years has probably noticed, the surrounding towns have built up quite a lot."

Nat sighed. Yeah, there seemed to be more people and houses around. But the town still didn't have a Loehmann's or a Sephora, which, in her mind, placed it squarely in the "backwoods" category.

"The state needs roads for those people to drive on," Dr. Steve went on. "The little one- and two-lane streets around here aren't cutting it anymore. The state of Pennsylvania has decided to build a state highway, and unfortunately, the plan that makes the most sense for the area cuts right through the center of Camp Lakeview."

The room was filled with indignant gasps. "They can't do that!" one of the older boys yelled.

"Yeah," a familiar voice agreed. Nat turned around and realized it was Adam, Jenna's brother. "Camp Lakeview owns this land, right? They can't just build a highway through it without your permission! So just don't give it."

Dr. Steve shook his head. "I'm afraid you're mistaken, Adam," he said sadly. "The government has a special right, called eminent domain. If something needs building that would be in the public's best interest, the government has the right to seize private property, as long as they pay for it." He sighed. "I'm very sorry, kids. We've been going back and forth with state senators all summer, hoping to work out a compromise. But it just doesn't seem possible. The state needs the road, and this is the only way."

"Why don't you move it?" Nat spoke up before she even realized she was thinking it. Stunned and a little nervous to hear her own voice rising above the crowd, she reached out for Logan's hand. He took hers and squeezed it. "I mean . . . does Camp Lakeview have to be in Pennsylvania? Maybe you could rebuild a totally awesome camp somewhere else and bring back all the same people."

Dr. Steve looked sad. "That's a nice idea, but Camp Lakeview has stood in this spot for ninety-two years. Moving and rebuilding would be expensive, and we'd lose some people, whether we wanted to or not. I'm sorry, kids." He sighed again and rubbed his eyes. "I'm very sorry to spring this news on you so late in the summer and without any options. Just know that we, the staff of Camp Lakeview, are just as saddened by this decision as you are." He paused and looked behind him, where Nat now realized some dining hall workers were arranging something on a table. Dr. Steve turned back to the microphone. "I know it's not enough to make it better, but we're going to have a little make-your-own sundae ice cream social to cheer ourselves up."

Dr. Steve gestured to the table behind him, now laden with huge tubs of ice cream, hot fudge, and all kinds of toppings. Nat barely registered that no one cheered. No one made a sound. It was maybe the first time in history that sundaes were met with silence at Camp Lakeview.

"Wow," Logan said. He turned to Nat, dropping her hand in the process, and Nat realized that she'd been holding on to it pretty hard.

"Wow," Nat echoed. "I just. I can't even . . ."

"What a shock," Logan went on, shaking his head in wonder. "I thought this place would be around forever. Long after we stopped coming, you know? I thought I could send my kids here."

Nat nodded. It was silly, she knew, but the first

thing she thought of was her and Logan, ten or twenty years in the future, sending their daughter off to camp. Now that wouldn't be possible.

"I just," Nat said again, but she couldn't continue. Her mind was racing. Ever since she and Logan had gotten back together, things had been so good between them. Better than good. Better than *ever*, actually. She knew they weren't "official" yet—they weren't calling themselves boyfriend and girlfriend—but she was so, so into him. All of Tori's talk about getting older and growing up made Nat wonder—could Logan be it for her? Could he be her first serious, long-term boyfriend?

Of course they hadn't talked about it. Not in so many words. Officially, they were still "testing the waters"—enjoying each other's company until camp ended and they had to make a decision. Still, Nat couldn't possibly imagine that Logan didn't feel the vibe between them. They were clicking so well, finishing each other's thoughts before the first person had even finished. He *had* to notice. And she was sure he felt the same.

Nat shook her head to clear it and a few tears leaked out of her eyes. "I just can't believe we won't be here next year, together," she said quietly.

Logan nodded solemnly and brushed her hair out of her eyes. "It'll be tough," he agreed. "I might go to this soccer camp. Honestly, I was thinking about it even before we found this out, but now it looks a lot more likely." He chuckled nervously.

It took a few seconds for that to register. *I was thinking about it even before we found this out.* Nat's head snapped up. "You were thinking you might not come back next year, anyway?" she asked.

Logan nodded, not picking up on the urgency in her voice. "Just something in the back of my mind," he agreed. "I mean, I love Camp Lakeview. But we're getting kind of old for it, and I might learn something useful at soccer camp."

Nat's mouth dropped open. *Something useful? Something more useful than spending time with her?* Was everyone around her secretly plotting to leave camp when she felt like she'd never survive the next summer without it?

She felt like Logan had reached into her exploded heart and ripped out what remained.

Nat heard sobbing and realized that a couple of the younger kids in Logan's bunk—he was a CIT this year—were crying. Logan leaped up.

"I'd better comfort these guys, Nat," he said with a sheepish smile. "I'll talk to you later."

Nat didn't reply. She got up quietly, trying to collect herself, and started walking back to her friends at 6B's table. *He doesn't want to see me next summer*, she thought without wanting to. *How can he feel the same way I do and not want to see me next summer?* Nat felt more tears well up behind her eyes and pushed the thoughts away. *Deal with that later. One crisis at a time.*

Approaching their table, Nat saw that all the girls from 6B were standing together in one big, messy group hug. Candace, Brynn, and Alyssa all seemed to be crying, and the girls who weren't crying seemed to be trying really hard not to. They all patted each other's backs, murmuring comforting things. Nat let out a sigh of relief.

This is where I belong.

Spotting Nat, Alyssa let out another sob and held out her arms. Nat rushed toward her and was immediately enveloped in the huge group hug. Nat felt the tears start again and wasn't sure whether they were the same ones she'd felt thinking about Logan or whether these were totally new, separate-issue tears. She decided it didn't matter.

It's all one huge mess.

After a few minutes of hugging and crying, Nat felt better. It was a huge relief to see that her bunkmates were as wrecked by the camp closing as she was. Finally, all the ice cream had been consumed—albeit reluctantly—and Becky suggested that 6B head back to the cabin.

Leaving the dining hall, Nat caught sight of Tori, who'd somehow remained just outside Nat's hugging range through the whole ice-cream-and-tears debacle. Nat saw that her friend's eyes were red from crying, although now, Tori was facing straight ahead, a determined expression on her face. Remembering that awkward conversation before dinner and Tori's bizarro suggestion that they go to *surfing* camp next summer, of all things, Nat sighed. *At least there's one upside to this whole situation,* she thought, running to catch up to her friend and grabbing her shoulder.

Tori whirled around, looking annoyed. "Oh, it's you. What?"

Nat tried to smile. "Well," she said with false cheer. "I guess the good news in all of this is, we can check out that surfing camp you mentioned next summer, guilt-free!"

For an instant, Nat thought she saw Tori's lip curl. But then Tori's expression slackened and she shrugged, looking away. "I guess," she replied.

"I guess?" Nat frowned. "You guess? I thought this was something you really wanted to do."

Tori's expression was cold. "Whatever," she replied. "I didn't want the whole *camp* to close to make that happen, you know."

"I know." Nat looked at her friend, stunned. "I never said you did."

Tori shrugged again. "Forget it," she said.

And she sped up, leaving Nat on her own.

For all her tears before, Nat wasn't sure what to do when they got back to the cabin and suddenly it seemed like *everyone* was crying. Maybe it was being in their own private space. Or maybe the girls were feeding off of each other's sorrow, realizing just how important camp had become to all of them. Whatever the reason, an hour later, all of 6B was sitting in a messy circle on the floor of Becky's room, passing around a box of Kleenex from Tori's care package.

"It's so weird," Alex was saying, wiping her eyes. "I've been coming to this camp as long as I can remember. I almost can't remember what I did with my summers before."

"I feel like I've known you guys my whole life," Val added, sniffling. "You guys *are* summer to me. What am I going to do without you?"

Jenna sighed, but Nat noticed that her eyes were dry also. "Don't worry, Val. It's not like we're going to die," she said sensibly. "We'll all stay in touch. We'll keep the blog going. We'll see each other again."

Brynn shook her head and reached for another Kleenex. "It won't be the *same*," she said, letting out a sob. "We won't all be together. And we won't be here. Even when we get together during the school year, it's something different. It's still fun. But it's not camp." She sobbed again.

Nat bit her lip. She felt tears behind her eyes again, and a part of her felt like one wrong move and she'd be bawling her eyes out with all of these guys. There would be no coming back from that. If she really let out all the sadness she felt inside, she was afraid she wouldn't recover for weeks.

Instead she cleared her throat and said, "But guys, we're getting older." She looked around the room and saw a sea of confused, wet faces. "Life goes on. Things change, right? Even if the camp was still open, we probably wouldn't be coming to camp much longer." She paused, glancing at Tori across the circle. "I mean, we're going to be in *high school*."

Nobody responded. That is, nobody said anything. But Nat heard a few sobs around the circle and saw a few people turn away with hurt expressions. It was like she'd said the worst-possible thing. Nat looked at Tori, expecting to see her nodding and agreeing.

But Tori was glaring at her. And after a few seconds, she looked away.

chapter

THREE

Jenna sat blinking in her bunk, slowly registering the warm sunlight streaming in through the windows. Somehow she'd slept a little later than normal. She sat up, rubbing her eyes, remembering the strange dreams that had plagued her the night before. She'd been back at school, but somehow the roles of all her friends back home were played by friends from camp. And they wouldn't talk to her. She'd done something to them—she forgot what it was now—and they were all mad at her. She remembered sitting alone at lunch in her dream, watching all her camp friends laughing hysterically as they sat at a table together.

Jenna looked around and dangled her legs off the edge of her bunk. *Whatever. Time to get up.*

In the bathroom, Jenna noticed that it was quieter than normal. Lots of her friends had tired-looking eyes, red-rimmed from crying the night before. Jenna sighed, remembering last night's emotional conversation as she stood under the shower. She'd been stunned to hear that Camp

Lakeview was closing, too, and she'd shed a tear or two at the sundae party. But something about her friends' reactions bothered her. There was letting out sadness, and then there was wallowing in sadness, and Jenna was afraid they were veering toward the latter.

She was dreading the next couple of weeks. She had the feeling it was going to be a pity party of epic proportions. Everyone crying and whining and pleading with the camp officials to open up again, blowing everything out of proportion and ruining their last two weeks of camp. Sure, it was a bummer that camp was closing. Didn't Jenna know that better than anyone, having come to Camp Lakeview every summer for as long as she could remember? But by spending all their time worrying about what they'd be losing, they'd completely waste the last two weeks of camp.

Once everyone was dressed and ready, it was a quiet procession outside and toward the dining hall.

"Hey," Jenna said to Priya, trying to lighten the mood. "So are you going to ask Johnny Swimcap to the social or what?"

Priya looked up and shrugged. "Why bother?" she asked. "If I thought I might be coming to camp next year, then maybe. But since this is all going to be over in a couple weeks, it seems silly. I should just hang out with you guys and enjoy the time we have."

Jenna sighed. *"Priya,"* she scolded. "You sound like you're going to die in two weeks, not leave camp."

"Leave camp for *good,*" Candace broke in. "There's a difference, you know."

Jenna couldn't help it. She rolled her eyes. "So

let me get this straight," she announced, looking around to address the whole bunk. "Camp is closing in a few weeks, so we're going to spend the last time we have crying and huddling and acting like we're at a funeral."

Brynn looked upset. "It *is* a funeral, Jenna!" she cried dramatically. "Camp Lakeview is *closing*. It's *dying*. And this is our last chance to say good-bye."

Chelsea looked sideways at Jenna. "Aren't you even a little bit sad?"

Jenna opened her mouth to answer, not sure what she was going to say. But before she could get any words out, a hand grabbed her arm.

She turned around and grinned. "David!" she cried, facing her boyfriend.

David's always-messy brown hair looked messier than normal, like he'd just gotten out of bed after a night spent tossing and turning. But his green eyes looked happy to see Jenna. "Hey," he said, unusually softly. "Wanna talk for a sec?"

He looked serious. Jenna nodded. "Sure." She glanced back at her bunkmates, still looking like they'd come from a screening of *Schindler's List*. "Um, I'll catch up with you inside, guys."

They shuffled past, and Jenna turned to David with a smile. "You're not going to try to trash-talk me about our soccer game later, are you?" she asked. She and David were both in the sports activity after breakfast and were usually friendly rivals. "Because I don't think *you* should be one to talk. I saw you kicking the ball in the wrong direction the other day. You're not exactly—"

"Jenna." David cut her off. Jenna was surprised; David was always jovial and happy to joke around. In fact, most of their conversations could probably be qualified as "joking around." It was part of what she liked so much about him.

Now he looked serious.

"What's up?" Jenna asked, concerned.

David sighed. "Are you okay?" he asked somberly, looking carefully into her eyes. "We haven't had a chance to talk since, you know, since—"

"Since the big announcement last night?" Jenna asked, her heart sinking as she realized that this was going to be yet another "Oh, no, Camp Lakeview is closing" conversation. *Et tu*, David?

David nodded. "Yeah." He gave her that serious look again. "I just wanted to talk to you, you know, and tell you that just because . . . I mean . . . it's going to be hard, but—"

Suddenly it hit Jenna. *"David,"* she interrupted him, giving him an incredulous look. "You don't really think I was worried we'd break up because camp is closing, do you?"

David looked at her, confusion playing in his eyes. "Okay . . . no?"

Jenna nodded. "Good. I mean, I like being at camp with you and getting to goof around and play sports with you and everything. But I'm not with you just because of camp and I wouldn't break up with you just because of camp, okay?"

David nodded, still looking confused. "Okay. But . . ."

"But what?" Jenna sighed and looked over toward the dining hall. Boy, she was hungry this morning.

"But . . . it's going to be *hard*, Jenna. We won't see each other as much. And I'm going to miss all my camp friends, and I'm sure you'll miss yours."

Jenna shrugged. "Sure. But we'll keep in touch."

David looked at her, stunned. It was like she was telling him she planned to build a spaceship and erect a new Camp Lakeview on the moon. The idea of *not* crying her eyes out over Camp Lakeview being no more seemed just that surprising to him.

"What's wrong?" she asked.

"Aren't you even a little upset?" he asked. "Isn't there anything you want to talk about, that you have on your mind?"

Jenna sighed again. If this was how the next two weeks were going to go, she might as well just go home now. Hadn't they already talked about it? How was talking about it *more* going to change anything? She shook her head in an exaggerated way. "*No*, David. Oh, wait. I take that back."

David looked a little hopeful. "What, then?"

Jenna grinned. "Pancakes," she said, backing away toward the dining hall. "I am *starving*. And I have to admit—I have pancakes on my mind, big-time."

Still, David didn't laugh. He didn't even smile. He just looked stunned.

He needs time, Jenna told herself. *Not everyone can deal with this stuff so quickly. He'll get to where I am.* Leaning in quickly, Jenna pecked David on the cheek and smoothed his hair. As soon as she moved her hand, his hair bounced back into position, which made her smile. "See you later, okay?" Not pausing for an answer, she started running into the dining hall. "In soccer practice! You'd better work on your sense of direction!"

She opened the double doors to the dining hall and slid inside, leaving him standing where she left him.

Jenna smiled as she sat down just as Dahlia was placing a plate of three gorgeous, golden brown pancakes in front of her. "Mmm-mmmm," she murmured, inhaling deeply. "I'm starving this morning. Aren't you guys?"

She looked around the table. Everyone was still looking depressed, but they mustered shrugs or little "yeahs" or "nos."

"You must be," Jenna went on, carefully spreading butter over the top so it all melted evenly. "It's a scientific fact, you know. Crying makes you starving."

A sharp laugh seemed to leak out of Val before she could stop it. "That's true, actually," she agreed, smiling a little. "It must burn a lot of calories or something."

"Great," Tori snorted, leaning in to butter her own pancakes. "We'll all be ten pounds thinner by noon."

A few people chuckled at that. Jenna smiled cautiously. *See? They're coming around.* "So who has exciting plans today?" she asked, taking a big bite of breakfast and chewing.

People glanced around at one another and shrugged.

"*I* have exciting plans," Sloan piped up, smiling as she sipped her juice.

"What are they?" Jenna asked. *It better be something good,* she thought. *Something to perk everyone up.*

Sloan shrugged, a mischievous glint in her eye. "Well, there's a lot to do," she said, "now that they announced camp is closing."

Jenna's heart sank. *No. We were finally talking about something else, and then Sloan has to bring up the closing again.* It wasn't fair.

"Come *on,* guys!" she cried. "Okay, it sucks that camp is closing, but I'm not about to spend the next two weeks talking about it nonstop, losing out on the great time we *could* be having!" She paused. "Don't you guys get it? Whether we cry and mope the next two weeks or whether we have the time of our lives, camp is *still* going to close. So let's have the same fun we've always had!"

She looked around at her friends, who were now looking sheepish and confused. "I wasn't going to mope for *two weeks,*" Gaby insisted, rubbing her red-rimmed eyes. "Maybe another couple *hours,* but that's my business."

Sloan was looking back and forth from Gaby to Jenna. "Hey, wait!" she cried. "You didn't let me finish."

Jenna turned to her. "Oh, sorry. Go ahead. Before camp closes, you want to cry by the lake one last time? Cry on a night hike one last time?"

Sloan shook her head. "There won't be any need for that."

Jenna nodded. "You got that right," she agreed.

"As for me, I'm going to spend each moment having the kind of fun I want to remember."

Sloan sighed. "*Jenna*. Everyone. Will you let me finish? There won't be any need to remember anything."

Nat looked over, frowning. "What does *that* mean?" she asked. "We all have memories we love. Memories we're going to want to keep forever."

Jenna wasn't totally sure, but she thought she might have heard Nat's voice crack when she said "forever."

Sloan shook her head again. "There won't be any need to remember," she said slowly, "because we'll *still be making memories*. Camp Lakeview isn't going to close, guys. Because I've come up with an awesome plan!"

chapter

FOUR

Tori frowned, pausing skeptically over her pancakes. "What kind of plan?" she asked. "I mean, Dr. Steve made it sound pretty clear-cut. The government wants the land. They give them the land. Period."

Sloan smiled. "But that's just it, Tori. The government is *for* the people, *by* the people, just like the Constitution says. We don't have to just sit here and take something we think is horrible! We should do like our parents' generation did when they thought the government was wrong—*protest!*"

A ribbon of chatter wove through the group as everyone reacted in different ways.

"Protest?"

"That's a great idea!"

"I think it's a pretty stupid idea."

"But it might work . . ."

Tori was quiet, biting her lip as she thought this over. Of course she'd seen footage of kids in the sixties and seventies, protesting the Vietnam War, the treatment of prisoners, all kinds of things. When her father watched certain movies or heard certain songs, he would get all nostalgic and start complaining to Tori that her generation was "too complacent—you have to get out there and fight for what's right! Don't you watch the news?"

Tori usually responded with a "Whatever, Dad." Her teachers and parents and all kinds of older people were always trying to teach her about the *power of the people*, how it was the responsibility of the population to police the politicians, etc. But she'd never been so personally affected by a government action. So if they did protest—could it really work?

"Look," Sloan was saying, "the state congress represents the people of Pennsylvania. The congressmen and congresswomen are people just like us! No more important and no less. Don't you think they'd want to know if we thought this decision was totally wrong?"

"Um," Nat inserted. "I'm not even a resident of Pennsylvania. Most of us aren't, actually. We couldn't vote in Pennsylvania elections even if we were old enough. So why should they care what a bunch of ninth-grade out-of-staters think?"

Sloan looked stunned. "Why *wouldn't* they?" she asked, shaking her head. "Look, you make it sound like they're kings and queens, people to be afraid of. But they're just people! Under democracy we're all equal! And if you want to know what's in it for them—if we told them how great Camp Lakeview is, wouldn't they want to preserve it? Maybe they'd like to send their own kids here."

Tori chewed thoughtfully. *She makes a good point,*

she thought. Somehow she'd never pictured the people who'd voted to close Camp Lakeview as mothers or fathers; she'd pictured them as being kind of scary, like Sloan had just said.

Alex spoke up. "That's all great, Sloan, but you're forgetting something pretty important."

Sloan looked surprised. "What?"

"What do we *do* to get their attention?" Alex asked, leaning in and looking around at her bunkmates. "Write letters? Call them at home?"

Sloan shook her head. "No, no, no. We stage a protest, guys! We go to the statehouse and stand outside with signs, chanting and telling everybody who passes by us what's going on! Haven't you guys ever been involved in a protest before?"

Everyone looked around at one another; almost everyone was shaking her head and shrugging.

"Jeez," murmured Sloan, taking a sip of her juice. "Well, it's about time you learn!"

Becky, who'd been watching all of this with a perplexed expression, looked even more concerned as she spoke up. "Guys," she said. "Um, this is a great idea, but I don't know how practical it is."

"Practical schmactical!" Sloan cried, waving her fork in the air. "Becky, we would work so hard on this! It'll be *great*. We could get a whole group together, not just us. We'll make signs and come up with chants; it will be an awesome learning experience! And maybe Dr. Steve would give us permission to use the camp buses to get there." She paused, taking a last bite of pancake. "You think?"

Becky sighed, still looking conflicted. She glanced over at Dahlia, who just shrugged with a "don't ask *me*" expression.

"It *would* be great," Tori spoke up, realizing as she said it that she really believed it. "We'd all work so hard, Becky. And I think—I think it would be *therapeutic* for all the campers to have a chance to at least *try* to save Camp Lakeview. Don't you think?"

"I totally think so," Val spoke up, nodding. "Becky, it's really hard to say good-bye to a place when you feel like you never had a chance to try to save it. This would be our chance!"

"Yeah." Gaby was nodding slowly. "And we would learn from it, too—about government and citizenship and how things work. Right?" She glanced at Chelsea.

"Right." Chelsea nodded. "Seriously, Becky, *please*. Please let us do this. Please?"

Soon everyone was chiming in. Girls who had looked skeptical before were now throwing themselves full-steam into pleading with Becky. Tori joined in, too.

"Please," she said, knowing that her words were probably tough to make out over the begging of every single one of her bunkmates. "I need to know we've done something. I need to at least try . . ."

Becky looked around at all the pleading faces and sighed, finally shouting, "Enough!" She held up her hands in a T shape and shook her head. "Truce, guys. All right, I get your point. Why don't you all think about this some more and then come back to me when you have a better idea how it's going to work. If it all makes sense, I'll help you make your case to Dr. Steve. Deal?"

Everyone's face broke into a smile. "Deal!" they all cried, looking around at one another in victory.

"Awesome," Sloan breathed to Tori. "I'm so glad she said yes. Now we have our work cut out for us!"

"Definitely," Tori agreed with a nod. Just then, she shot a look at Nat. To her surprise, Nat was the only girl not smiling—in fact, she looked like she'd just seen a ghost. She poked at her pancakes with her fork for a few seconds before sighing and pushing them away.

What's up with her? Tori wondered.

"Okay," Sloan began, settling back on a bottom bunk with a pen and a big pad of paper. "I hereby call to order the first meeting of Camp Lakeview Citizens for Change! Who wants to be first?"

"Citizens for Change?" Jenna asked.

Sloan nodded. "One very *specific* change, but change nonetheless."

"I like it," Brynn spoke up. "It's very . . . dramatic. It makes a statement."

"But what is that statement?" Jenna asked, twirling a finger around her ear, the universal signal for "crazy!"

"Jenna, hush," Alex admonished her friend, leaning forward into the circle of campers. "Let Sloan talk. The name of our group is kind of a moot point right now, at least until we get the okay to make our protest."

"Hear, hear!" Sloan agreed, pumping her fist in the air. "But that's permission that we're *sure* to get. I just know this bunk is full of amazing ideas for our protest. So let's hear them!"

The girls all looked around at one another. Tori

was holding her notebook, in which she'd doodled a couple ideas for signs, but she didn't want to be the first to speak. The truth was, she wasn't all that sure what a "protest" consisted of, anyway, besides lots of marching and shouting.

"I have an idea," Alyssa said quietly, holding up a sketchbook. "For me, Camp Lakeview has been all about artistic expression—it's really freed me up to be creative and make some beautiful pieces. And judging from my art classes, I think it's done that for a lot of other people, too."

"And?" Chelsea asked impatiently, but Sloan held up her hand.

"Let her finish."

Alyssa smiled shyly. "I thought we should incorporate art into the protest. Instead of just bringing signs, we can create new paintings to show how beautiful the grounds are and how they mean different things to different people. We can even bring some of the best pieces from the art classes this year to show the politicians what amazing things are being made here."

Sloan was nodding now and lots of the other girls were, too, smiling and glancing at one another. "That's awesome," said Sloan. "It gives the people passing by something concrete to look at, something that shows how much the camp means to us in a totally different way than our signs will. Great idea, Alyssa."

Alyssa blushed and smiled.

"Who else has an idea?" asked Sloan.

Brynn confidently raised her hand.

"Yes, Brynn?"

Brynn stood up and smiled. "I think it would be great if we could *entertain* the people who watch us," she said, looking around at each girl. "Instead of just waving our signs and chanting, we can *show* the congresspeople what we're talking about by performing a funny skit." She paused. "Humor is a really powerful thing. So I could write a skit about how coming to Camp Lakeview changes one girl's life. Like, she suddenly has all these friends, plus she learns how to swim and draw and use a compass . . ."

"I've been coming here three years now," Val said with a laugh. "I *still* don't know how to use a compass."

"That's because you have no sense of direction," Gaby admonished her.

"All the *more* reason I need to know how to use a compass!" Val giggled.

Jenna grinned and put her hand on Val's shoulder. "Well, you've got two more weeks," she offered. "Let's make this a priority."

"A-*hem*." Brynn rolled her eyes, but she was smiling.

"Right," Sloan said in a businesslike way, turning back to Brynn. "I think that's an *awesome* idea. Let's do it, Brynn. Get to work on that skit."

Brynn broke into a satisfied smile. "Awesome. I will."

"I have an idea," Gaby announced, looking around.

"Go ahead," said Sloan, posing her pen over her pad of paper.

"Well, when I first came to camp, I could be a little bit . . ." She paused. *"Strident."*

Alex was watching her in amazement. "Does that mean bossy?"

"Okay, bossy." Gaby shrugged, looking a little chastened. "But being around you guys really changed all that for me! And that one time where I lied about my brother and tried to leave camp . . ."

Priya shook her head and rolled her eyes. "Don't remind me."

"It really taught me a lesson," Gaby continued. "Since then, I've been such an awesome person! Don't you agree?"

Everyone laughed. "I would say you've been *better,*" Alyssa said cautiously.

"Well, whatever." Gaby made a dismissive gesture and rolled her eyes. "My point is, going to Camp Lakeview makes you nicer. Can we do anything with that?"

Brynn looked confused. "Like, a skit?"

Gaby shook her head. "No, nothing that complicated. More like, we're all just really *nice* and nice to each other and the people we meet . . . and then at some point, when we're done talking to them, we could be like, 'You see how I'm so much nicer than you? That's because of Camp Lakeview.' "

"Um," Sloan began awkwardly. "Um, I'm not really sure—"

"Here's an idea," said Tori, jumping in to save Sloan. "It seems like Camp Lakeview has meant something different to everyone. In fact, we could all probably tell

a personal story of how we've changed since we've been coming here. So what if we made those stories part of the protest? We could take turns telling stories of what camp means to us."

Sloan nodded slowly. "I like that," she said. "You're so right, Tori—what better way to show people how important Camp Lakeview is than to *tell* them?"

"Awesome," Candace agreed. "I'll start writing out my story."

"Me too," agreed Alex.

"That's about the cheesiest thing I've ever heard," muttered Jenna. She was staring into her lap.

Sloan turned to Jenna with a stunned look. "What?"

"I mean I'll *do* it," Jenna backtracked, playing with the end of her ponytail. "No offense. But don't you think it's kind of . . . sappy?"

The usually easygoing Sloan was getting a little crease of annoyance between her eyebrows. "How would *you* do it?" she asked Jenna.

Jenna sighed. "Um . . . I wouldn't," she said honestly.

Several people gasped in surprise. Then there was the dull murmur of people turning to each other and making under-the-breath comments. Before things could get really awkward, though, Nat spoke up.

"Guys," she said in a thin, stressed-out voice, "not to agree with Jenna, but . . . is this really worth it?"

She paused, and eleven sets of eyes swung toward her.

"I mean . . . Dr. Steve said they'd already tried

negotiating with the state congress. They've already been turned down. What if we devote all our energy to this, spend our last two weeks working on it, and it's *still* not enough?" She paused, biting her lip. "What if we still can't save Camp Lakeview?"

Everyone seemed to be glancing around at one another, considering Nat's words, trying not to get sad.

"I just worry," Nat went on, "that we're throwing ourselves into this to distract ourselves from the truth. That this is really our last summer. All of a sudden."

There was total silence for a few seconds. Everyone seemed to be thinking that through, and all the smiles and excitement from earlier seemed to drain from the room like someone had pulled a huge stopper out. Tori looked around at her friends. She knew they were all thinking some version of what Nat had just put into words. Of course they realized that the protest might not work. But somehow, to hear Nat say it out loud—it made Tori really—*angry*.

"Of *course* it's worth it!" she shouted, and all eyes turned to her. "Come on! Natalie! *Anything* that has even a little chance of saving Camp Lakeview is worth whatever we can do. Don't you believe that? I mean what, are we too lazy to make a few signs, write a few statements?"

A murmur of agreement went around the room. Tori realized that her little outburst had come out sounding more enthusiastic than angry, but she could tell Nat had read the anger in her voice. She turned away, picking at her sweater and staring at the wall.

"I'm not!" Chelsea was saying. "Come on, guys,

let's work our butts off to save this place!"

"The state congress may be powerful," Sloan agreed with a grin, "but there's no power greater than the power of the people! Let's *do* this, guys!"

More and more people spoke up to agree with Tori. By the time they got ready for bed, Sloan had five pages filled with ideas, and they each had individual assignments to start pulling the protest together. When they presented their ideas to Becky, she seemed pretty impressed. "I'm not promising anything, guys," she said, biting her lip as she read over their ideas. "But I think this is worth running by one of the powers that be."

The girls all cheered. As they disbanded to wash their faces and change into their pajamas, Tori knew that she should feel great right now, victorious. But instead she felt awful—like something had crawled into her heart and died. She brushed her teeth, washed her face, and changed into her nightgown without talking to anyone. As she was heading back to her bunk, Tori passed Nat, who looked at her with a questioning expression.

Tori didn't know what to say. She walked past Nat and climbed into her bunk, pulling her sleeping bag over her head.

chapter FIVE

"Omigod, the greatest idea for our protest came to me in a dream last night." Priya put down her fork and looked around at her bunkmates, all eagerly shoveling mac and cheese into their mouths. It was lunchtime the next day.

"What is it?" asked Sloan. "I left my notebook in the bunk, but I can write it down on my napkin."

"Okay." Priya paused dramatically, looking around at everyone again. "We all wear black."

There was a moment of silence.

"Uh-huh," Chelsea said finally. "And?"

"*And?* That's it! We wear black! Like we're at a funeral, get it? We're in mourning for Camp Lakeview!"

Gaby wrinkled her nose. "Doesn't that send the wrong message? Like, the camp is already dead?"

Priya rolled her eyes. "If you take it *literally*. Jeez."

Sloan looked thoughtful. "Actually, I like it. I like it." She pulled a pen out of her pocket and jotted something down on her napkin. "Black will make us look more put-together and serious. Good thinking, Priya."

Priya smiled, satisfied. "Anytime."

Becky took a sip of bug juice and cleared her throat. "Actually, guys," she said, looking a little hesitant, "I've been thinking about your whole protest idea."

Nat felt her heart squeeze. She'd been watching the whole conversation with a feeling of dread. As much as she wanted to save Camp Lakeview, the very idea of the protest freaked her out—because if she let herself believe even for a second that the camp could be saved, that left her open to get her heart broken all over again. She hadn't spoken to Logan once in the last twenty-four hours, but she'd been replaying their last conversation in her head nonstop since they'd spoken the night of Dr. Steve's announcement. *I might learn something useful at soccer camp.* And what would happen to them as a couple when they couldn't be together at camp? Would their romance shut down as the buses pulled away for the last time? Would she ever see Logan after that?

Nat gulped. The whole idea was too painful to dwell on, but she knew she had to face the future head-on and not distract herself with great ideas that might not lead anywhere . . . like this protest. Was it even worth trying? A big part of her was hoping that Becky would tell them right now that the protest was a bad idea. At least then, Nat would have the next two weeks to come to terms with losing Camp Lakeview—and maybe Logan—forever.

All of the other girls, though, looked like it was

Christmas morning and Becky was about to start handing out presents. "And?" Chelsea asked eagerly. "What have you been thinking?"

Becky looked serious for a few seconds, then her face cracked into a smile. "I've been thinking you guys have some really good ideas," she admitted. "And you obviously put your hearts and souls into this. I think you should run your ideas by Dr. Steve and see if he'll support the protest and give you permission to use the buses and other camp resources. Without his help, this protest will be really hard to get off the ground."

Nat could barely make out the last part of Becky's sentence with all the shrieking.

"Omigod!" cried Brynn. "Thank you so much."

"This is amazing," Sloan agreed with a huge smile. "Thank you so much for believing in us, Becky. I promise to make you proud."

Becky nodded. "Just do your best," she replied. "I've made an appointment for you guys to see Dr. Steve at three thirty this afternoon. So you'll probably want to work out before then who says what and how you want to present your ideas."

Sloan nodded. "Definitely. From this point on, we're in crunch mode!"

"I'll present the skit idea!" Brynn yelled, just as Alex asked, "So should we write out a skit to perform?"

"There's no *way*," Gaby piped in. "How could we come up with a skit good enough before three thirty? Tell you what, I can help with the skit presentation."

"But it was my idea!" Brynn cried.

"Wait a minute, wait a minute," Alyssa broke in.

"How should we handle the artwork? Should we bring some to the meeting? Should we make up a sample sign?"

"Yeah, definitely!" cried Candace at the same time Tori replied, "No, there's no time."

"Guys," Becky broke in, looking a little concerned and, if Nat was right, relieved not to be in charge of planning this presentation, "I'm going to leave you all to work this out. Dahlia and I are going to go outside to do some paperwork, okay? Just keep your voices down!"

"Okay." Sloan looked a little disappointed to see her counselor go but turned back to her bunkmates with a businesslike expression. "Guys. Let's get serious. We're going to have to work together to make this presentation work, and I think we should all be involved. So why don't we go around and everyone can say how they'd like to help, and we can go from there?"

Gaby looked disappointed. "All right."

Brynn nodded somberly. "Cool."

Nat was stunned when Sloan turned to her with an expectant expression. "Nat, let's start with you. What would you like to do in the presentation?"

Nat opened her mouth, but no sound came out. She sat up straight and tried to pull herself together. "Well . . . I . . . um . . . wow."

"You could talk about how camp made you humble!" Chelsea cried out. "Like you're the daughter of this big movie star and thought you were all cool, but then—"

"Chelsea," Sloan said sharply, holding up her hand. "Let the girl talk."

Nat stared at the table in front of her, trying to think. What did she want to do in this presentation? What would be her ideal thing to work on?

"Um . . . can I get a . . . *small* role?" She looked hopefully up at Sloan.

"*What?*" asked Alex as the others started murmuring and turning to one another.

"What do you mean, Nat?" Sloan asked patiently. "Why do you want a small role?"

"I guess . . ." Nat sighed, trying to put it into words. *I don't want to get my hopes up?* But she knew she'd get creamed for that. "I—"

"You've been really negative about this whole thing," Tori cut in suddenly, an accusatory tone to her voice. "Last night, you were saying this wouldn't work. And now you barely want to be part of the presentation to Dr. Steve!"

All eyes turned to Nat again.

"Yeah," Gaby agreed, looking thoughtful. "That's true! And you haven't had *any* ideas for the protest at all."

Nat looked at her best friend. (*Former* best friend? She couldn't tell anymore.) Before this week, Tori had been the person she counted on most at Camp Lakeview. She would never get all accusatory with Natalie, especially not in a public place like this. What was going on with Tori?

"It's like you don't care if Camp Lakeview stays open," Tori was saying now, a crease of anger between her eyes. "Is that it? Why do you want Camp Lakeview to close?"

"I don't!" Nat cried, and to her embarrassment, her voice cracked on the last word. She swallowed and closed her eyes, trying to regroup. When she opened them, Tori was still watching her with the same angry expression. Something snapped inside Nat. She couldn't understand why Tori was being so mean to her, but she wasn't going to put up with it anymore. "Tori, *I* care about Camp Lakeview a lot. Unlike you! You were all ready to leave it for some *surf* camp before the big announcement."

Gasps went around the table. "Is that true?" Brynn asked. "Tori, you were going to leave us?"

Tori's face was bright red now. If she'd looked angry with Nat before, she looked *furious* now. "I had a *private* conversation with Nat about a letter I'd gotten from my cousin," she explained tersely. "She invited me to come to surf camp with her next summer. That's all."

"But you were all hyped up about it!" Nat accused. "You wanted to *go*, and you wanted to take me with you."

Everyone looked stunned. "Well, if that's true, Tori," Val said, "I guess this whole camp-closing thing works out well for you."

Tori shook her head, angry tears glistening in her eyes. "I was considering it. I hadn't made any decisions yet." She paused, glaring daggers at Nat. "You should talk, Natalie! You say camp means the world to you, but you don't want to help save it, and you're always ditching all of us supposed best friends to go hang out with your not-even-boyfriend."

Nat gasped. She was *going there* with the Logan thing? Was this seriously the same Tori who'd been her best friend these past years?

"You're a hypocrite, Tori!" she cried. "You're trying to pass yourself off as all gung ho about saving camp, but *you didn't even care enough to come back next year!*"

Tori's eyes were cold and hard as she stared back at Natalie. "Seriously, Nat," she said in a low voice, "how much of your big sadness about camp is about losing *camp* and how much is about losing Logan?"

Nat felt like her heart might explode again.

"Guys," Jenna cut in finally, "let's calm down, okay? So Tori was thinking about leaving next year. It's not the biggest deal. People decide not to come back every year."

Tori shook her head. "What matters is right now. The protest. And Nat needs to step up."

"Maybe *you* need to calm down, Tori," Nat retorted. "Since if the protest doesn't work and camp closes, that'll just give you an excuse to do what you wanted to do in the first place."

Angry murmurs ran around the table.

"Seriously, though," Jenna spoke up, raising her voice to get heard. "Seriously, though! How many of you guys were coming back next year even if the camp stayed open? Be *honest.*"

The table grew quiet. Everyone turned to everyone else, looking, it seemed to Nat, for traitors. She looked at Tori, long and hard.

But Tori was now stubbornly staring in the other direction.

The tension at the table was thick, and Nat felt both eager for someone to cut it by speaking up and scared that if someone *did* admit they might not have come back next year, it would turn into a riot. She felt like all of her friends were in the emotional red zone: waaaayyyy too keyed up over the news of camp closing to react normally to anything.

Suddenly there was a loud whistle. Nat jumped.

"Lunch is over!" called one of the boys' counselors. "Everyone off to your next activity!"

Everyone turned back to face the table, openmouthed.

"Great," said Sloan with a frustrated shake of her head. "We were too busy fighting over who *cares* enough about camp to come up with a plan to actually save it. Good work, guys."

Nat looked at Tori, who looked sincerely guilty. "Hey," Tori said to Sloan, "I'm sure it will work out. We all know what we want to do. And we'll all work our hardest on the presentation."

Sloan just sighed. "Everyone think about what you want to say," she said tersely, shoving her napkin into her pocket. "We'll probably have a few minutes waiting for Dr. Steve."

As they all got up and started heading off to their activities, Brynn put her hand on Sloan's shoulder. "Hey," she said. "Think Tim Gunn. We'll just 'make it work.'"

Sloan smiled warily. "I sure hope so."

Nat was walking toward the lake with her towel slung over her shoulder when her vision darkened, a pair of warm hands covered her eyes, and she smelled the familiar cozy *boy* smell of her favorite boy in the world: Logan.

"Guess who," he said from behind her, making a pathetic attempt to make his voice high and girly.

Nat felt herself smiling for the first time in what seemed like weeks. "Um . . . Mary-Kate Olsen?"

"Guess again."

"Amy Winehouse?"

He made a buzzer sound. "Nope! Hel*lo*, she's British."

"Hillary Clinton."

"Oh, boy." Logan sighed a big, showy sigh and used his normal voice again. "You know what? I'm going to help you out here. Who has two arms and two legs, a bunk of little kids to care for, and adores you?"

Nat felt her stomach turning liquid at that last part. "Um . . . Dr. Steve?"

Logan laughed, dropping his hands and spinning Nat to face him. "Oh, man. Is there something going on between you two that I don't know about?"

Nat made a face. "Don't be a perv. Dr. Steve adores everyone at this camp."

Logan sighed and shook his head. "That was a pretty poor showing."

Nat smiled. "I should've guessed it from your Bubblicious breath."

Logan grinned. "Dude, it's watermelon. Want a piece?"

Nat shook her head.

Logan shrugged. "That's cool." He stood back

and looked at her. "Why so serious today? Where's the usual Nat sparkle?"

Nat felt a little pit open up in the bottom of her stomach. *Why? He has to ask why?* "Um, I guess I'm still just rattled by the news that camp is closing."

Logan nodded slowly, still not seeming to get it. "That's deep."

Nat sighed. "Aren't *you* upset?" she asked in a frustrated tone, then softened her voice. She didn't want him to feel like she was accusing him of not caring enough—the way Tori spoke to her about this lately. "I mean, you seem to really like being a CIT. You like being outdoors. You like—" *Me*, she thought fiercely. But her throat seemed to close up, keeping her from saying it.

Logan nodded. "Yeah, yeah, of course I do. And of course I'm a little upset." He paused, putting his arm around her shoulders. "I just don't want to dwell on it, you know? And you shouldn't, either, Nat. It's not going to make you feel any better to be all sad about it twenty-four seven."

Nat shook her head, amazed. Boys were really something else. Could Logan seriously talk himself out of being upset like that? Just because it didn't make sense?

"I know that," she said. "I'm just sad. I can't talk myself out of feeling sad when that's how I feel."

Logan nodded, reached to take her hand, and gave it a squeeze. "That's cool. But what's making you so sad? Are you going to miss this lake? These bunks?"

Nat's eyes started to burn. *You*, she wanted to

say. *I'm going to miss you and you're not going to miss me. Don't you get it?* But she just shook her head and looked away. "Everything."

"Aw, Nat." Logan put his hand back on her shoulder and gently rubbed it, leading her over to the lake.

Suddenly Nat realized something: the protest! Logan had no idea that they were working on a protest—that there was a chance camp could be saved!

"Hey!" she cried, stopping short and turning to face him. "I forgot to tell you. My bunk is working on something—something *big* that could save Camp Lakeview!"

Logan smiled. Nat felt her heart melt a little at the sight of it—she'd grown so fond of that smile in the last couple weeks, the way it slowly moved over his face and then lit up his eyes. "That's great, Nat," he said with a nod. "Maybe that will help you feel better."

Nat swallowed. "Make me feel better?" she asked. "It's bigger than that. We could save the camp."

"Sure, sure," Logan agreed, walking a few steps toward the lake. "And even if you don't, it gives you something to focus on."

Nat stepped forward, grabbing Logan's hand and turning him to face her. "Focus on?" she asked. "We could save the camp, Logan. Don't you get that?"

Logan looked at Nat, but something was missing from his eyes. Nat could tell just by looking at him that their saving camp didn't mean the same thing to him that it did to her, just like she could tell he didn't understand why she couldn't just stop herself from being sad.

"I get it," he was saying. "It's great, Nat. Let's swim."

But Nat felt like she couldn't move her legs from this spot until she said more. "If we saved camp, we could be together again," she said quickly, hoping that her voice didn't break. "We could have one more summer, at least."

Logan looked away, then looked back at Nat. It was still missing—the thing she wanted more than anything else to see in his eyes. "Great," he said lightly. "We'll play it by ear. Come on, Nat. Let's have fun."

Nat felt her body go light, and she followed him over to the lake without stopping again. But she knew she wasn't going to have *fun*.

It had been only days since Dr. Steve had made his big announcement, and it seemed like she couldn't remember what *fun* even felt like.

▲ ▲ ▲

"Okay, okay, okay." The normally Zen Sloan was looking flustered as she flipped through the notebook where she'd jotted down their protest ideas. The girls of 6B were all sitting in a little waiting area outside Dr. Steve's office, trying to prepare for their big presentation. "Brynn—you're going to talk about the skit idea?"

"Roger," Brynn said, without looking up.

"Who?" Sloan asked, flustered.

"*Yes.*" Brynn looked up and smiled. "I'll present the skit idea, Sloan."

Sloan nodded. "Great. Now, Gaby—you're going to talk about our personal stories?"

Gaby made a face. "Are we still doing that?"

Sloan nodded. "Sure. Why not?"

Gaby shrugged. "It just seems like *certain people* don't think camp was that important in their life at all."

Sloan sighed. Tori frowned at Gaby.

"That's not true," she insisted. "Just talk about the story thing, okay?"

Gaby rolled her eyes. "Fine."

"Great," said Sloan, quickly flipping through her notes. "And—who's going to talk about art? Alyssa?"

Alyssa glanced over, a nervous expression on her face. "Do I have to?"

Sloan shook her head. "No, you don't have to. But you did a good job presenting to us last night."

"*You're* not Dr. Steve," Alyssa replied. "I got nervous enough in front of you guys."

"Okay." Sloan looked around the group, touching her index finger to her lip. "How about . . ."

But she didn't get to finish. Rebecca, Dr. Steve's secretary, appeared in the doorway and smiled at the girls. "Ladies, Dr. Steve is ready for you," she said, and retreated back to her desk.

"*Crap*," Sloan whispered, slamming her notebook shut. Then she looked around at her friends, trying to look positive. "I mean—great! Do you guys feel good? Are we ready?"

Alex looked unconvinced. "I—guess so?"

Sloan nodded. "Awesome," she said, standing up and walking toward Dr. Steve's door. "Let's go."

They all followed Sloan, if not exactly eagerly. Dr. Steve was waiting for them, leaning back in his chair with his hands clasped behind his head. "Ladies of 6B!" he said with a warm smile as they filed in. "To what do I owe this pleasure?"

"Well," said Brynn, at the same time Chelsea cried, "Social justice!" and Sloan explained, "We have an idea to run by you, Dr. Steve."

Dr. Steve looked from one girl to the other, clearly confused. "Okay," he said. "I gather that . . . well, okay. Why don't you girls just continue?"

Sloan took a deep breath and sent a warning glance to her bunkmates: *I'm handling this one.* "As I was saying," Sloan said, "we have an idea."

"We want to protest!" Gaby cried, pushing through Val and Alyssa to get closer to Dr. Steve.

"Yeah," Priya said. "We want to go all the way to congress! We want to make our voices heard!"

"Power to the people!" added Brynn.

Dr. Steve surveyed all of them, looking like he didn't quite know what to make of all this. "Run that by me again?" he said.

"*Ahem,*" said Sloan, shooting her bunkmates a warning look. "As Gaby so eloquently put it, we want to try to save Camp Lakeview. We want to arrange a protest to let the state congress know how upset we are about this decision!"

"They should know how much Camp Lakeview means to us," Alex put in. "It's not just some *camp* you can *close*. It's our camp!"

Dr. Steve's mouth dropped open. He looked like he wasn't quite sure what to say next. "Well—" he began finally.

"We're going to bring art!" Tori added, glancing at Sloan with a wink. "The best and brightest paintings from the art classes, plus new paintings and drawings of the camp grounds!"

"And we're going to *act!*" added Chelsea.

Dr. Steve furrowed his eyebrows. "Act?"

"What Chelsea means is, we're going to write a skit," Brynn explained. "We'll perform it during the protest."

"It'll be funny!" Val added.

"But serious," Candace cautioned.

"But more funny than serious," Val said.

"But really, what they mean is touching," Jenna said. "Touching and poignant and not at all, like, cheesy."

"We're going to show them how nice we are!" Gaby threw in, jumping up to be seen over her bunkmates' heads. "All day long we'll be, like, really nice, and when they ask why we're so nice, we'll be, like—"

"We're *not* doing that," Chelsea corrected her.

Gaby pouted. "I thought we were undecided."

"It's obnoxious," Chelsea said.

Gaby glared at her. "I am way too nice to respond to that."

Nat cringed. She'd known they weren't exactly *prepared* for this meeting, but still, this was going way worse than she'd feared. What if Dr. Steve said no and put an end to the protest before they even really started? She wasn't sure anymore whether that would be a good thing or a bad thing.

Dr. Steve, who'd been watching the girls'

presentation with a stunned, slack-jawed expression, seemed to pull himself together and sit up in his chair. "Girls," he said, "can one of you summarize very briefly for me what you plan to do? Because I'm getting confused."

Sloan glared at her bunkmates. "I can summarize!" she offered. "Dr. Steve, what we'd like to do is borrow the camp buses to travel to Harrisburg to stage a protest. We would protest Camp Lakeview's closure. In front of the congress building."

Dr. Steve nodded slowly. "And this protest would consist of . . ." he prompted.

"Signs!" cried Nat.

"The skit I told you about," Brynn added.

"Personal stories," Priya spoke up.

Val nodded. "Like, we would all take turns telling what camp means to us," she explained.

"Um, not *exactly*," Gaby corrected her. "More like, we would say what we were like before camp and how much better we are now."

Alyssa looked uncomfortable. "I don't know if that's exactly how I'd put it—"

"We'd have chants, too!" Alex cried, trying to cover up her friends' disagreements.

"What would the chants be?" Dr. Steve asked, a smile playing on the corners of his mouth.

The girls all looked at one another. They hadn't even really discussed chants; Alex had just thrown that out there to change the subject. Still, they knew they had to say something.

"Heck, no . . . we won't go . . . if you close Camp Lakeview?" Tori asked.

Dr. Steve broke into a full smile at that, but he quickly covered his mouth with his hand, regaining his serious air. "Girls," he said. "I'm sure you understand, if I support this protest, if I let you use the buses to go into another city with a huge group of fellow campers—I have to be confident that this protest is organized down to the minute."

The girls all glanced at one another, nodding slowly. Nat was surprised to feel a twinge of dread in her stomach. *He's going to say no*, she realized. *Camp is really going to close. Logan and I are really going to break up.*

Dr. Steve continued, "If this presentation was supposed to show me that Camp Lakeview taught you to overcome your personality differences and work as a team to really plan something . . ."

The girls all sighed. They knew what he was going to say.

"Then that was a pretty poor showing." Dr. Steve looked from girl to girl, an expression of disappointment on his face.

The girls were silent, dejected. They all stared at their hands, the floor, anything to avoid looking at one another or at Dr. Steve. *Tori and I blew it*, Natalie thought guiltily. *Now we've lost our chance to save Camp Lakeview because of our stupid argument at lunch.*

"However." Dr. Steve looked at Sloan. The girls all perked up, turning to one another and back to Dr. Steve, surprised to hear him add anything else.

"I feel that this is a noble goal, saving Camp Lakeview, and that if you pull it off, the younger kids could learn a lot from it." He smiled. "And I can see that you're all very worked up about this, probably because Camp Lakeview is so important to each of you, in different ways."

Sloan nodded. "Definitely!"

Dr. Steve nodded, too. "I'm going to give you three days," he said, looking around at each of the girls again. "This time, I want you to come up with a great protest idea, and I want you to present it to me so that I feel totally confident in your abilities. Got that?"

"Got it!" Alex cried.

"All right." Dr. Steve nodded toward the door. "You're all dismissed. And remember: work *together!*"

"Wow," Sloan murmured at dinner, sticking her fork into her spaghetti for what seemed like the hundredth time. "Just, wow."

"I know," Becky agreed. "You guys have quite a task ahead of you."

"It has to be the perfect protest," agreed Brynn, looking thoughtful. "Totally organized, without a dull moment." She sighed. "Guys, we are going to have to work our *buns* off on this one."

"I kind of can't believe we thought we could organize it during lunch," Tori said.

"Totally," Priya agreed. "This is going to be the only thing we think about for the next forty-eight hours."

Nat picked at her food. She was glad they got another shot at planning the protest. But she still felt horribly nervous—that they wouldn't convince Dr. Steve, that the protest wouldn't work, and most of all, that this time next summer, she would be sitting alone in Central Park, missing Logan like crazy.

"Uh-oh," she heard Jenna say, looking at something right behind Nat. "Look who's coming for a visit."

Nat spun around. *Oh, no.* It was Lainie—a girl who Nat had almost become friends with, until she realized that Lainie could be shallow and two-faced and that she had a *huge* crush on Logan, who she called Christopher. (Which was actually his first name, but Nat liked Logan sooo much better.)

Lainie moved to the side, and Nat gasped—speak of the devil, Logan was following along behind her. What were Logan and Lainie talking about? Nat felt her stomach drop a hundred feet. *Just when you thought things couldn't get any worse . . .*

"Hi, ladies!" Lainie called in her loud, girly voice, sidling up to their table with Logan close behind. "Look who I found, sitting all by his lonesome out on the porch."

Nat turned to Logan, who was wearing a sheepish expression. "I was with a camper," he explained. "He . . . um . . . the spaghetti tonight didn't agree with him."

Several of the 6B girls dropped their forks onto their plates for the last time.

"Anyway," Lainie said with a big smile. "Christopher here told me something *wild*. He told me that you guys— cute little 6B—are planning, like, some crazy protest to save the camp or something?" She looked around at the girls, wearing an incredulous expression. Nat knew the intended message was, *Silly little 6B actually thinks they can make a difference?*

"We *are* planning a protest," Sloan affirmed. "It's really in the early stages right now, and we don't know for sure whether Dr. Steve will approve it. But we're going to work really hard on it."

"That is *precious*," Lainie gushed, patting Sloan on the shoulder. "Well, I'll tell you what. If someone is trying to save Camp Lakeview, I want to be a part of it. Sign me up to help!"

Nat turned to face Lainie, stunned. "Are you kidding?"

Lainie shrugged. "Of course not," she said, smiling warmly at Logan. "I wouldn't want to miss a minute of camp. After all . . ." She glanced from Nat to Logan and back again. "Who knows what could happen in a school year?"

Nat felt her stomach clench. So that was it: Lainie wanted to save camp because she thought Nat and Logan might break up, and she wanted to be around in case her beloved "Christopher" became single again. Nat's chest burned with anger. *She wants to help us? Well, she can help us by getting out of here and not touching our protest with a ten-foot pole,* she fumed to herself.

But Sloan was smiling her warm, crooked smile. "That's great, Lainie," she said. "We've planned to spend all our free time tomorrow in the auditorium, working on the protest. Sort of whoever's free at a given time can head over there, and then in the evening, we'll all work together to rehearse."

Lainie smiled a huge, sickly sweet smile. "That sounds perfect!"

Nat groaned inwardly. This wasn't all hard

enough—now she had to work with Lainie, too?

As she was about to put her head down on the table and moan, though, she felt Lainie staring at her. "What a cute top, Nat," Lainie said, lifting a ruffle from the top of Nat's cotton cami. "What is that red shape, exactly? A heart?"

Nat glanced down at her top and felt her face growing hot. "That's spaghetti sauce."

Lainie laughed, a grating, tinkly sound. "Cute," she said, flashing a dark look at Nat. As soon as it came, though, it disappeared, hidden behind a fake smile. "See you girls tomorrow! Come on, Christopher. I want to show you my new purse, back at our table."

Logan flashed an apologetic look at Nat and mouthed, *See you tomorrow in the auditorium?* Nat just nodded. Her head felt heavy. In fact, everything felt heavy.

Never had a task seemed so impossible as getting this protest planned well.

chapter SIX

Jenna ran like her life depended on it, across the sports field, past the mess hall, along a row of cabins, and finally to the auditorium. She was just getting out of a nature hike, and she knew her bunkmates had been working on the protest all day.

Throwing open the auditorium door, Jenna noticed that inside it was fairly quiet and organized. After their messed-up presentation the day before, she'd been expecting chaos. But all of the girls were sitting in a big group in the audience, conferring quietly as Gaby stood onstage at the microphone.

"Sorry, Gaby," Sloan called finally. "That was good. Start up where you left off?"

Gaby smiled a big, theatrical smile. She lifted the microphone to her lips. "And then I came back for my second summer at Camp Lakeview, thinking I was already perfect. I mean, I had great friends, great grades, boys loved me, and I was really popular back home. But just because you're popular doesn't mean you don't have a lot to learn.

When I got back to camp, I realized—"

"Hold on, Gaby," Brynn called out from the audience. "Um, I think we want to keep these pretty short so we can get a lot in. Maybe cut the part about how great you were back home?"

Gaby made a face. "But it's *important* to the *story*. Isn't it more important to tell a good story?"

"I don't think it's that important, Gabs," Alex called. She realized what she was saying and sighed. "I mean, yes, I think it's important to tell a good story. But I don't think *that* piece was that important to *your* story. You know?"

Gaby scowled. "How would you know? It's my story. I haven't even finished it yet."

Sloan held up her hand. "All right, truce," she said, looking from Alex to Gaby. "Gaby, why don't you keep going, and if it needs to be cut, we'll figure it out at the end. We have to make this work, guys. We don't have time to argue."

Brynn and Alex glanced at each other and nodded reluctantly, and Gaby shrugged and brought the mike to her lips again.

"Anyway, when I got to camp, I realized that I still had a lot to learn. I . . ."

Jenna zoned out as she walked over and took a seat beside her friends. It was siesta time, so almost everyone was there. She noticed that Tori and Nat were sitting in the same row with Val between them, but Nat was chatting casually with Val, and Tori was obsessively reading over her notes and making changes. The two of them never made eye contact. Jenna rolled her eyes.

What was *up* with those two? They were usually best friends, but now they were acting like worst enemies. She just hoped they wouldn't take down the whole protest with their fighting.

Turning away from Nat and Tori, Jenna looked at her own empty lap. Truthfully, she hadn't prepared for this rehearsal at all. Would they be able to tell?

"... and as I sat there, back in my bunk, surrounded by my campmates who loved me enough to forgive me for lying to them, I realized that it was wrong to lie to people. It's wrong to make up stories to make people want to be your friend. The most important thing is to be yourself and be a nice person. And I have been honest and nice ever since." Gaby finished her anecdote and smiled hugely at the assembled audience. Then she took a bow.

"Nice job, Gaby," Sloan called. "We made some notes, but we can go over them together. Overall that was great."

Gaby smiled like she wasn't surprised. "Thanks."

"No problem." Sloan looked back at the audience, and her eyes landed on Jenna. Jenna looked down at her hands, trying to look like she was puzzling something out.

"Jenna, you haven't been able to come by till now. Do you have something you want to perform? We can go over it and give you notes."

Jenna felt her heart squeeze, but she didn't want to show her friends she was nervous and unprepared. "Sure," she said. "Um, it's a little rough."

"No problem," Sloan replied with a smile.

Jenna forced herself to smile back. As she walked up to the microphone, she spotted David ducking through the auditorium doors. Jenna had told him about their protest saga, and he, Logan, and Adam had offered to swing by and help plan whenever they had a free minute. *Great*, Jenna thought with a frown. *He's just in time to catch my inspired performance.*

She picked up the mike and thumped her finger on it, creating a big *thunk* sound. "This thing on?" she asked.

"Yeeesss," chorused her bunkmates.

"Okay." Jenna paused, trying not to get distracted by David, who was smiling at her and giving her the thumbs-up as he slid into a seat in the third row. "Um. Camp Lakeview. Riiiight." She paused again. "Well, when I first came to Camp Lakeview, I was feeling a lot of pressure, because my whole family had gone here, you know, including my twin brother, Adam." She glanced at her friends in the audience. Brynn looked unsure, but Sloan smiled encouragingly. "I felt like I had a lot to prove, so I kind of acted out a lot and pulled a lot of pranks and stuff." Sloan nodded and made a gesture with her hands implying that Jenna should expand on that. "Um, all kinds of pranks—like, leaving rubber snakes in beds, stealing all of another bunk's toilet paper, crazy stuff." Sloan nodded again and gave Jenna a look that said, *And?* "But after a while I made some really good friends and realized I didn't have to prank it up just to stand out from my family. So that's how Camp Lakeview made me a better person. The end."

Jenna smiled. *Not bad for no preparation at all.* She

glanced at David, who gave her a sort of halfhearted thumbs-up. *What's that about?* Then she turned to her bunkmates, who were looking at each other with concerned expressions.

"That was great, Jenna," Sloan said with a stiff smile, but Jenna could see confusion in her eyes. "I think what it's missing, though, is the emotional connection. We want to really convince people that Camp Lakeview is *needed*—that it has a *huge* impact on kids' lives. So maybe you could get more, like, emotional."

Jenna stiffened. "So you want me to fake tears?"

"Not *tears*, exactly," Brynn said, spreading her hands in the air. "But maybe you could talk more about how you felt when this stuff happened, how good it *felt* to have friends, that sort of thing."

"Um," Jenna muttered, feeling really annoyed and not sure why. "Okay. I guess I'll try it again." She paused and then looked into the audience. David smiled again, nodding encouragingly.

"When I first came to Camp Lakeview," Jenna announced, projecting in a loud, theatrical voice, "I was a *sad* girl. I felt all kinds of *pressure* to live up to my brothers and sisters, who had come to camp before me. I cried all the time, and when I wasn't crying, I was pranking. Pulling pranks was the only thing that relieved the *emptiness* inside me." She paused and looked down at Brynn. "Like that?"

Brynn looked unsure—like she wasn't sure whether to be encouraging or mad. Jenna could tell that Brynn realized she wasn't being totally serious. But everyone was so keyed up about this presentation, she wasn't sure what to do.

"Um, *kind* of," said Sloan, glancing back at Brynn like, *I'll handle this.* "Maybe you could be a *little* less dramatic? More like, 'I felt really down and depressed,' and less, 'there was all this *emptiness* inside me.' You know?"

Jenna sighed. "Okay. Let me try it again." She paused, made a big show of shaking herself out, took a deep breath, and spoke into the microphone again. "When I first came to Camp Lakeview," she said, "I was down and depressed. I thought I could never live up to the example my brothers and sisters had set. To make myself feel better—because I was really sad—I pulled pranks." She paused, letting her voice crack a little on the word "pranks." Then she looked down, like she was collecting herself, and wiped a fake tear from her eye. "But now—" she continued, letting her voice crack again. "*Now*—" She dissolved into fake sobs. "Oh, now I'll never be sad and depressed again! Because I've discovered the power of good friends and *Camp Lakeview*." She held the mike for a few more seconds, sobbing fakely. Then she punched her fist in the air, pretending to totally recover. "Save our camp!" she yelled.

Jenna looked out into the audience with a smile. She was sure everyone would appreciate her injecting some lightness into this super-serious rehearsal. But instead, everyone was staring at her in openmouthed silence. Even David looked uncomfortable—and he *always* laughed at her jokes.

Brynn shook her head. "So," she said finally. "This is funny to you?"

Jenna rolled her eyes. "Oh, come on, Brynn," she

coaxed. "Lighten up a little, will you? It's like you all think we're at a funeral. 'Whatever will we do without Camp Lakeview?'" She shoved the mike back into its holder. "These little sob stories, it's like we're auditioning for *America's Next Top Model* or something. Who has the saddest backstory? Don't you think it's a little cheesy?"

"*Jenna,*" Sloan broke in, "we're trying to change people's minds in a very short amount of time, okay? So we're going for emotional. You *do* think camp has changed your life, don't you?"

Jenna shrugged. "Of course it has," she muttered, catching David's eye.

"Then why don't you want to save it?" demanded Brynn. Her sharp tone told Jenna that she was still angry.

Jenna wasn't sure how to react. She really hadn't meant to make anyone mad. "Who says I don't want to save it?" she asked.

"You showed up here totally unprepared, and instead of seriously trying to make it work, you made a big joke." Jenna was surprised to hear Alex's voice piping up out of the crowd. "If you want to help save camp, why didn't you work on writing out something? Why haven't you made any suggestions for the protest?"

Jenna felt her mouth drop open. She couldn't believe this. Her friends were totally turning on her. "*Look,*" she said. "Maybe *I'm* the only person around here who's facing reality! Maybe I didn't want to spend hours writing out some cheesy script for myself because I realize that this stupid protest probably won't even work!"

A gasp went through the crowd. "I can't believe you would even say that!" cried Val.

"You *guys*," Jenna pleaded. "It's not like I said I hoped that would happen. I'm just being realistic here! What are the chances, seriously, that this will work?"

"I think our chances are great!" Candace cried at the same time David stood up and caught Jenna's eye.

"Hey, Jenna," he said loudly. "Can I talk to you for a sec?"

Jenna looked at her boyfriend in surprise. David was never that forceful or serious. They were totally comfortable around each other and, on the rare occasions they didn't agree, were able to joke about it. So it surprised Jenna to see David looking truly upset.

"Sure," she said softly, and followed him offstage and to a quiet corner in the back of the auditorium. Behind her, her bunkmates moved on to the next true confession, and Alyssa nervously took the stage.

David turned to face her, still not quite meeting her eye. He glanced over to the side of the auditorium and sighed. "What's up with you?" he asked finally.

"Not much," she said lightly, still hoping to make him smile. "What's up with you?"

He sighed again. "What's up with *me* is I'm worried about my girlfriend. She's acting like she really doesn't care about camp at all and making a lot of people upset."

Jenna scowled. She couldn't help it. She knew David wasn't trying to antagonize her, but still—why was everyone ganging up on her? Just because she wasn't ready to slit her wrists at the thought of Camp

Lakeview closing? Wasn't her way of dealing with it the *healthy* way? Moving on, facing reality, all that?

"Well," she replied, an edge to her voice, "what's going on with *me* is that everyone's ganging up on me, *even* my boyfriend!"

She paused. David looked a little guilty.

"Seriously, Dave," she continued, "do you think I'm heartless or something? I'm not. I'm a realist. And I think this plan is doomed—there, I said it."

David sighed. He looked like he'd been slapped across the face. "Even if you think that," he said finally, "why would you say it?"

Jenna was dumbfounded. "Because it's the *truth*?"

David shook his head, like he was trying to clear it. "The truth hurts," he replied softly. "Seriously, Jenna—don't you want the camp to stay open?"

Jenna paused. She tried to imagine coming back to camp next year, and she felt a little twinge in her chest, like it was making her nervous to even imagine it. "I'd like a lot of things," she replied. "Like, I'd like to win the lottery, I'd like my boyfriend to stop giving me grief—but I know those things probably aren't going to happen." She paused. "I'm trying to prepare everyone, David."

David was staring at the floor. He looked up at her, green eyes peering under his long eyelashes. "You're bringing everyone down," he said quietly.

Jenna sighed. "I can't help that."

David shifted, ready to leave the conversation. "And you're hurting a lot of feelings," he added, his voice going a little hoarse.

Jenna felt a squeezing in her heart. Suddenly she saw how upset David looked. "What do you mean?" she asked.

But he was already walking away. He turned and said over his shoulder, "Do you *really* not care if camp closes and we don't get to see each other next summer?" he asked.

Jenna opened her mouth to speak, but no sound came out. *He thinks I don't care*, she realized. *He thinks because I'm not worried the camp will close that I'm not worried about losing him.* Jenna started to run after him, but just then, a loud voice cracked the low murmur of voices coming from the stage.

"Hello, hello," Lainie greeted them, strutting into the auditorium and raising her hands over her head, as if to say, *Aren't you happy I'm here?* "Sorry to make it over here kind of late, girls. I've been meaning to come by all day, but my bunk has been kur-*azy*, you understand." She paused. "Or maybe you don't, not being CITs. Anyway—let's get this party started! How can I help?"

"Hi, Lainie," Sloan said warmly, standing up from her seat in the audience and waving her notebook. "We're just glad you could make it. The more voices heard, the better!"

Lainie snapped her gum. "Tell me about it," she agreed. "Well, why don't you start by letting me hear some of your voices? Let's take it from the top. Show me what you've got so far!"

Sloan turned to Brynn, both girls looking caught off guard. Jenna had been at rehearsal long enough to realize that the protest wasn't anywhere near ready yet. Still, Brynn shrugged and flipped a few pages back in her notebook.

"Okay," she said. "We talked about starting with a song—come up onstage, everyone!"

The assembled campers—it was about two-thirds of their bunk, plus David and Adam, who had come in while Jenna and David were arguing—slowly, unsurely made their way to the stage. Brynn was holding her notebook open to some original lyrics she had written.

"Okay, guys," she whispered to them as they formed a cluster onstage. "This is to the tune of 'America the Beautiful.' Just follow my lead."

She started singing:
"O beautiful for endless fields
For chats that last all night
For swimming in an azure lake
And bird hikes at first light!"

Brynn's voice was loud and high, but nobody else quite knew the words, so a low murmur was the best they could do. Jenna looked at her friends uncertainly. When the song finally—mercifully, it seemed to Jenna—ended, Brynn flipped a page in her notebook.

"Okay," she said. "Now Alyssa, Val, you guys bring up the paintings and talk about artwork."

Brynn gestured to the rest of the campers to step down off the stage. Alyssa and Val looked at each other like two deer in the headlights.

"Um," Alyssa said. "Okay . . ."

They ran down the steps to the stage and grabbed a few paintings from the first row, then ran back up. Alyssa turned to the audience with a strange, frozen smile.

"My name is Alyssa," she said very slowly, "and I've been taking art at Camp Lakeview for three years now."

Alyssa went on to talk about the importance of creativity in young people's lives, blah blah blah, showing details from this painting and that painting and trying to explain how Camp Lakeview nurtured that creativity. She was really nervous, Jenna could tell, and would sometimes lose her train of thought with an "ummmm . . ." or a "yeah, so, anyway . . ."

Finally Val jumped in and wrapped up. "So as you can see from these paintings," she explained, "there are many different ways of seeing, and Camp Lakeview helps us all find our special way."

She nodded forcefully and then gestured back to the still freaked-out Alyssa. They each carried a few paintings down the stairs and off the stage.

"Okay," said Sloan, consulting Brynn's notebook. "Next up are some personal stories. Gaby, why don't you—"

"Way ahead of you," Gaby replied smoothly, slipping in front of the microphone. "Good morning," she said too close to the mike, amplifying her voice to a ridiculous degree. "My name is Gaby Parsons, and I am a better person than I was three years ago because of Camp Lakeview."

As Gaby continued, Jenna, sitting in the front row now, turned and watched Lainie watch them. She was shocked to see Lainie facing down into her hand, her shoulders shaking—was she *crying?* Was that even possible? *Wow,* Jenna thought, shaking her head. *I guess our little protest is a lot more powerful than we thought.* But then Lainie shifted and lifted her face, and a loud bark of laughter rang out over the auditorium, loud enough to drown out Gaby's too-loud soliloquy.

"HA! Omigod . . . HA HA HA HA HA HA ohhhhh . . ."

Gaby stopped, startled, and shot a death glare at Lainie. Everyone else turned around slowly, looking puzzled and a little upset. Lainie was still laughing, but her fit seemed to be dying down.

"Oh, man," she said, wiping mascara from her eyes. "Man. That was . . . priceless."

Brynn let the silence grow for a second before she spoke. "What's so funny, Lainie?" she demanded finally, hardness in her voice.

Lainie shook her head. "Do you even have to *ask?*" she replied. "Did any of you see that? Were you watching? Do you know what that was?"

Sloan kept her voice even as she replied, "It was a *protest.*"

"No." Lainie shook her head and laughed again as she got back to her feet. "It was a train wreck."

Sloan, Brynn, and all of the assembled campers of 6B, plus Adam and David, all exchanged glances. Jenna could see that everyone was upset, and she felt pretty upset herself, which surprised her. This wasn't *her* protest—it wasn't planned the way she would have planned it, and it was way too emotional for her taste. But still, it infuriated her that Lainie made fun of it.

"Who are you to waltz in here at four thirty in the afternoon and call it a train wreck?" Jenna shouted in Lainie's direction. "What do you know about protests, anyway?"

Lainie just laughed. "I know what works," she replied. "The people you're protesting for aren't going to be experts in what makes a good protest, either. They'll just know what moves them. And I can tell you, that didn't move me—except out the door."

Sloan was shaking, she was so upset. "You don't know what you're talking about!" she cried. "You know what makes a good protest? Heart! And we're *all* pouring our whole hearts into this. If we stand up for ourselves and tell congress what we truly think and feel, there's nothing more powerful than that!"

Lainie shrugged. "If you say so, honey." She slipped out of her row of seats. "All I know is, this isn't worth my time."

Brynn watched Lainie leave, still looking angry but also curious. "What would you change?" she called after Lainie.

Lainie turned on her heel and laughed. "Everything?"

Brynn shook her head. "Seriously, though. You tell me what you didn't like. What's wrong with what we've got?"

Lainie looked thoughtful. "Okay," she said. "For one, I couldn't hear a thing you said."

Brynn nodded. "Okay. That's fair. But we'll bring microphones."

Lainie sighed. "But that's not all. That almost

makes it worse. If they can *hear*, they'll hear how ridiculous you sound. Nothing you guys are saying makes sense, Brynn. That song? Amateur hour. The art thing? Totally mumbly and obvious. And Gaby's story?" Lainie laughed. "I don't think it's playing the way you want it to play."

Brynn sighed and turned to Sloan, who still looked furious.

"Get out of here, Lainie," Sloan insisted. "You're not helping us, fine. We don't need your help."

Lainie shrugged. "Suit yourself." She pivoted and, in a few seconds, was gone.

There was silence in the auditorium. Nobody seemed to know how to react. It was like Lainie had popped their balloon; they could try to keep playing with it, but they all knew something was wrong.

"It's a good protest," Sloan said quietly. "What does she know? We'll make it work."

But Brynn was staring at the floor, her mouth set in a tight line.

"She's right," Brynn said finally. "Guys, this isn't working." She sighed. "We have to come up with a great idea—something to save this protest, fast." She paused. "Or we may never get the chance to save Camp Lakeview."

A quiet murmur went through the crowd as the girls reacted. Jenna was surprised, but she knew Brynn was right. They'd have to come up with something. For now, though, she needed to talk to David—even though she wasn't sure what she was going to say.

But when she turned around to where David had

been standing, he was already gone. She caught sight of his red T-shirt as the doors closed behind him.

Jenna shivered. Suddenly the auditorium felt a little chilly.

chapter
SEVEN

Dear Michael,

Sorry I haven't written in so long! It's not because I don't miss you—I miss you like crazy. It's just that it's been nuts here and I've been super-busy. A few days ago, we found out that Camp Lakeview is scheduled to close next year. Something about the state needs a new highway, blah blah blah. Anyway, we've been totally messed up over it—let's just say we've gone through LOTS of Kleenex in the past couple days! But one of my bunkmates, Sloan, came up with a plan, and now we're going to go to the state capitol to protest the camp closing! I'm so excited, but also stressed out. We have to come up with a really good plan for the protest if our camp leader is going to let us go. And of course, I'm kinda freaked out about camp possibly closing and having to leave all my friends . . . but that won't matter if our protest works.

Oh, I almost forgot, I got a letter from Cassie the other day talking about her little trip to surf camp! It sounds like she had a really good time. She actually was saying how she thinks I should go with her next year—but of course if this whole protest thing works out, I won't. I belong at Camp Lakeview with all of my friends.

Love ya,
Tori

"Okay." Brynn took a deep breath and put her notebook down on the table in front of her. "I hereby call to order our official brainstorming session for the protest to save Camp Lakeview! First, the rules of brainstorming. *There are no stupid ideas!* Got it? We never know what might work."

Jenna nodded. "Fair enough."

Gaby raised her hand. Tori looked over at Brynn and thought she looked a little hesitant as she said, "Go ahead, Gaby."

Gaby smiled. "I thought we could really make a statement with our protest. Like, you know those 'truth' ads on TV about smoking, where all these people pretend to be dead bodies in front of the cigarette companies?"

Sloan nodded. "Sure, okay."

"Well, I thought we could all dress in white and then pour ketchup all over us to look like blood! And then we could lie in the street with a big sign: CAMP LAKEVIEW'S CLOSURE IS KILLING US."

Brynn was speechless. Sloan glanced over at her and poked her with her fork. "Are you writing this down?"

"Um," Brynn muttered, scrambling into action. "Sure. Great. Um, thanks, Gaby. Who's next?"

Tori looked around the table at her bunkmates. Priya raised her hand. "Well, people really like puppies, right?"

Tori glanced around at her bunkmates, who all nodded. *Hard to argue with that.*

"I thought maybe we could borrow some

puppies," Priya continued. "From a local shelter or a pet store or something! It would bring attention to us, and then maybe we could give them out to people who promised to support us?"

"Wow," breathed Brynn.

"I know!" Priya smiled. "It's out there. But you have to admit, it would definitely draw some attention!"

Brynn nodded slowly, scrawling in her notebook. "Okay," she said. "Who's next?"

They slowly went around the table, everyone shouting out the three ideas they'd been charged with coming up with the night before. To Tori, none of the ideas really made a lot of sense—even her own, to team up with a local boutique and have giveaways, or to learn the congresspeople's favorite songs and play them, or to get their parents involved. Her heart sank as she realized that nobody had thought of an idea that might save the protest. What on earth could they do?

"All right," Brynn said finally, looking over the ideas in her notebook. "Good effort, guys. We have a lot of really . . . interesting . . . ideas here."

"Oh, who are you kidding?" Chelsea cried, shaking her head over her waffles. "These ideas are all crazy. We don't have anything here that makes sense or would make the protest work!"

"Come on, Chelsea," Sloan cautioned, leaning over to look at Brynn's list. "There are a few usable ones here. What about mine?"

Chelsea looked indignant. "To all dress up like mimes and just cry?"

"Weep silently," Sloan corrected.

Chelsea made a face. "We're so doomed."

Tori spoke up. "Why don't we pick out the few that are actually . . . doable? Like, we could actually accomplish them by tomorrow."

Brynn nodded. "That's a good idea. Okay. I'll read them all off . . ."

A few minutes later, they had a list of four ideas.

"All right," Sloan said. "We've got it down to Brynn's idea to write the protest into a musical, Jenna's idea to make it into an athletic competition, Nat's idea to have a fashion show, and Candace's idea to give away candy."

"Um, technically," Candace broke in, "we could give away candy with whatever else we end up doing. You know. We just need to buy a couple bags of Snickers or something."

Sloan nodded slowly. "Fair enough," she said.

Brynn sighed. "Should we vote?" she asked. "Everyone in favor of the athletic competition?"

Jenna and Alex raised their hands.

"Everyone in favor of the fashion show?"

Nat, Priya, and Chelsea raised theirs. Tori was a little tempted to vote for that one but eventually decided that she was still too annoyed with Nat to support her idea.

"Everyone in favor of the musical?"

Tori and all the remaining girls raised their hands. They had a clear winner.

Brynn looked around the table, nodding. She didn't exactly look excited that her idea had won. In fact, she looked kind of . . . tired.

"Wow," Brynn breathed. "Okay. I guess that's it, then. We turn our protest into a piece of musical theater." She turned to Sloan. "Overnight."

Sloan looked nervous, but she smiled tightly and nodded encouragingly. "Right," she agreed. "I'm sure we can do it! You're such a theater pro, Brynn. This will be a piece of cake."

Brynn looked less than convinced, Tori thought. She looked to Becky. "Um, can I stay out of my activities today to work on this?" she asked.

Becky nodded. She looked like she was feeling a little sorry for Brynn. "Do what you need to do, Brynn. And let us all know if you need any help."

Brynn nodded. "Okay." She looked around the table. "I'm going to get started right away, I guess. If you guys could come by to help whenever you have free time, I'd really appreciate it. And plan on meeting during siesta again to rehearse." She paused. "I think we're going to need a *lot* of rehearsal."

The whistle that signaled the end of breakfast sounded, startling everyone back to reality. Tori stood up slowly and gathered her things. She had archery now, with Nat. They hadn't spoken at all since their little blow-up at lunch two days ago, and she wasn't sure what would happen now—would they keep giving each other the silent treatment? Or would a couple hours away from the rest of the bunk give them the time they needed to make up?

She glanced over and saw Nat staring moonfacedly over at Logan's table, biting her lip.

Tori shoved her chair back under the table with a little too much force. Then she took off, deciding not to wait on her friend.

▲ ▲ ▲

"Nice try!" Kara, one of the counselors who taught archery, appeared behind Tori and gently took the bow from her. "What you want to do is angle it just a *tad* more to the right. Like that. That will give you a little more control."

Tori sighed, trying to mimic Kara's stance. The truth was, she couldn't care less about hitting the target today. Her thoughts were with Brynn, holed up in the auditorium trying to write a full musical in about six hours. Or at least half of her thoughts were there. The other half kept wandering off into the future, where Camp Lakeview was closing and Tori was headed home . . . to her boyfriend . . . and a new school year . . . and maybe surf camp beyond that . . .

Tori pulled back and then released the arrow. It went more to the right, all right—missing the target by ten feet and landing limply in the grass.

"Wow," breathed Kara.

"Maybe I'm just not cut out for this," Tori suggested.

Kara shrugged. "Maybe not," she agreed. "But remember, this might be your last chance to master archery! When Camp Lakeview closes, where are you going to learn how to shoot a bow and arrow?"

I won't, Tori thought. *And is that a bad thing?* She shrugged. "I'll keep trying, Kara."

Kara nodded. "Don't give up."

As Kara wandered off and Tori aimed another arrow, she noticed another archer miss the target entirely—off to the left this time. She raised her head and realized that it was Nat. Of course. They were both hopelessly inept at anything that required aim. Just a few days ago, they would have been standing side by side, giggling together at their combined lack of talent. But that was before their fight. Tori narrowed her eyes, watching Nat aim another arrow. She couldn't deny it: She was still mad at Nat. For one thing, she'd totally tried to make Tori look bad in front of their friends, bringing up the private letter from Cassie and trying to make Tori look like some kind of huge traitor when it was *Nat* who didn't seem to care at all about saving Camp Lakeview. Nat had barely made a peep at the protest rehearsal last night, and her ideas this morning, even the fashion show one, had obviously been cobbled together minutes before breakfast.

Nat's second arrow still missed the target by a good six feet. Nat shook her head and laughed at herself. In doing so, she noticed Tori watching her and stopped, staring for a second. Tori quickly glanced away, but it was too late: Nat was on her way over.

"Crap," Tori whispered under her breath, trying to look absorbed in reloading her bow and arrow. But within seconds, Nat was standing behind her.

"Hey," she said in a friendly voice.

"Hey," Tori replied without turning around, trying to make her voice cool.

"So, um, that was weird the other day." Nat

stayed her ground, crossing her arms and planting her feet in a way that seemed to say, *I'm not moving until you talk to me.*

Tori sighed: She was trapped. "Yeah," she replied in a breezy tone. "How about that?"

"It just kinda stinks," Nat went on, her tone still friendly, "because we've always been really close at camp, right? I mean, we're practically best friends."

Tori shrugged. She *so* wasn't ready to make up yet. "If you say so."

That did it. An edge crept into Nat's voice. "If I *say* so?" she asked. "Tori, what's wrong with you? Why are you treating me like something you scraped off the bottom of your shoe?"

Tori sighed and turned around. "I don't know what you're talking about," she replied, even though she knew exactly what Nat was talking about.

"You're mad at me," Nat went on, looking at Tori carefully. "I get that much. You've been strange ever since you told me about that surfing camp. I just don't understand why."

Tori looked up, meeting her friend's eye. She shrugged again.

"Is it because camp is closing?" Nat asked. "Is it because I'm spending too much time with Logan? Spit it out, Tori, so we can make up and enjoy these last two weeks together."

Tori's eyes flashed. "Wrong and wrong," she said, turning away to watch the other kids shoot at the target. "I'm not upset about that stupid surf camp because right now the only thing on my mind is saving

Camp Lakeview." She paused, turning back to Nat. "You remember that, right? This big protest you can't be bothered with?"

Nat glared at her. "I care about it just as much as you do!"

"Really?" Tori let out a cold chuckle. "Because you just said, 'Let's enjoy these last two weeks,' like that's a definite thing. And you barely said a word at rehearsal last night or breakfast just now. It really seems to me like you don't think Camp Lakeview is worth saving."

Nat's face fell. "Of course I do!"

Tori shrugged. "Well, then, maybe you should stop moping around like someone ran over your Jimmy Choos and focus on saving camp. That's what's wrong, Nat—I'm tired of seeing your miserable face sucking all the enthusiasm out of our protest!"

Nat's mouth dropped open. It was like Tori had said the worst thing she could have possibly said. "You don't think I care about Camp Lakeview?"

"If you do, you have a funny way of showing it."

Nat glared at Tori. "I care more than you could possibly understand! I care so much, I can't even *think* about this protest because to think about it means acknowledging that it might not work! Do you *get* that?"

Tori shook her head, slowly and deliberately and said, "No."

Nat sighed. "Of course, why would you? It's not the same for you—you haven't been coming to camp for all three years. It's just something new and fun to

96

you. That's why you were so ready to ditch it for Camp Ukulele or whatever."

Tori felt her jaw drop. She couldn't *believe* Nat was going there. So Tori didn't love Camp Lakeview as much as Nat did—just because she'd missed that first summer? Of all the insane—

"All I'm saying is, you'd better snap out of your funk," Tori hissed at her friend, leaning closer. "Because this is *it*, okay? This is your last chance to save the camp you love so much. So pull it together!"

With that, she spun on her heel and stomped away.

▲ ▲ ▲

"Okay, guys." Brynn stood before all of 6B on the stage of the auditorium, holding a sheaf of ragged-edged notebook paper and looking like she hadn't slept in three days (which was pretty amazing, Tori figured, because she knew Brynn hadn't looked like that this morning). "I have a . . . a working draft. I have an *outline* of how I would like the musical to go."

Sloan, who was standing next to Brynn onstage, turned and gave her shoulder a little supportive squeeze. "Of course we don't expect it to be finished, Brynn," she said warmly. "As long as we have a good starting point . . . as long as it's *entertaining* . . ."

Brynn gulped and glanced down at her scribble-filled pages. "Oh, it'll be entertaining," she replied.

"Great." Sloan turned to her bunkmates and smiled. "Let's get started, guys. This is going to be *really* great! Creativity in action!"

"Right," Brynn muttered.

Tori and all of her assembled bunkmates stood up and made their way to the stage. Tori noticed that Nat was standing way on the other side of the group and seemed to be avoiding eye contact with her. Nat was barely saying anything to anyone, though occasionally she would respond to a direct question from Alyssa or Val. For a second, Tori felt a twinge of guilt for getting so angry at Nat that morning. The truth was, she'd missed Nat these past few days—all their gossip sessions, secret chats, and private jokes. But something kept Tori from going over to her friend now. It was like a wall had gone up between them. She knew she was being hard on Nat, but she couldn't shake herself out of it. It was like *everything* had gone wrong this past week—the news of camp closing, the drama of the protest, and losing Nat as a friend. Tori wished she could just hit one big rewind button and make it all not true.

But she couldn't.

"Tori."

Tori turned around to see a slightly manic-looking Brynn shoving some crumpled pages at her.

"You're going to play Little Teri Fishbottom, a kind of rough, uncultured girl who comes to camp and gets exposed to culture and art and totally remakes herself. Can you do a Cockney accent?"

Tori stared at Brynn. "Little . . . Teri . . . Fishbottom?"

Brynn sighed. "Do you know what Cockney is?"

Tori shrugged, trying to look helpful. "I could maybe do a southern accent? Sort of?"

"Good enough." Brynn shoved the crinkled pages at her and moved on to Priya. "Priya, you're going to play Elgatha Moss, who comes to camp really embarrassed because she has purple skin but then learns to be herself and feel accepted. You have a big eleven o'clock number called 'Violet Like My Heart.' Can you belt?"

Priya looked confused. "Can I wear a belt?"

Brynn shoved some pages at her. "Next!" she cried, moving on to Jenna. "Okay, Jenna, you play Orphan Sally . . ."

Tori lost track of her friends' roles as she started reading over Brynn's notes. It looked like they all were playing outsiders and weirdos who learned to express themselves and feel accepted through camp, except for Brynn, who played the counselor. Together they all sang the big finale, called "We Love Camp," which according to Brynn's notes was supposed to have some pretty elaborate choreography. Tori looked over Brynn's lyrics:

"We love camp
Though it's sometimes damp
We don't need a lamp
We vamp
At camp!"

Tori didn't know much about musical theater, but she had a very uncomfortable feeling in the pit of her stomach.

Suddenly, the main doors swung open on their squeaky hinges, letting in a ray of white sunlight that framed a dark silhouette. All of the girls squinted, trying to make out their new (and only) audience member.

Sloan gasped.

"Lainie," she breathed.

"Hi, ladies!" Lainie whipped off her designer sunglasses and shoved them into the pocket of her gauchos, smiling widely. "I heard a rumor at lunch that you were revamping your protest based on my comments. So I figured, since they're making an effort, shouldn't I do them the favor of coming to check it out? Maybe I'd be willing to help again!"

Brynn stared at Lainie like she'd seen a ghost. "Oh god," she whispered.

"That's great!" Sloan cried enthusiastically, gesturing to a prime seat in the audience. "We're just about to do a dry run of Brynn's new musical that she wrote based on the camp experience! Have a seat, check it out!"

Brynn gulped and clutched some ragged pages to her chest. "It's *really* rough."

Lainie just smiled. "Well, of course it is, silly!" She sat down in the center of the fifth row. "I don't expect you to write a totally polished musical in twenty-four hours! But I'm sure the *flavor* of your talent shines through."

Brynn didn't say anything. She swallowed again. Then she turned to her bunkmates. "Um," she said. "Okay. Act one, scene one. It's me, Tori, and Candace."

All of the other girls slowly made their way to the wings of the stage.

"Tori," Brynn instructed in a whisper, "climb on Candace."

"*What?*" Tori whispered. But Candace was already

crouching down, gesturing for Tori to hop on her back, piggyback-style.

"Who are you playing?" Tori whispered, reluctantly climbing on.

Candace grabbed Tori's ankles and slowly stood up. "The bus," she replied. "I have the first song."

Brynn stood in the center of the stage, making a big show of looking eager and nervous. Candace started walking toward her—slowly, hampered by carrying Tori.

Candace began to sing.

"I am the bus
No need to make a fuss
I carry campers every summer
I know they won't find camp a bummer . . ."

When it ended, Tori wasn't sure how long it had gone on. It was like she had entered a fugue state where she knew she had read her lines, knew time had passed, but when Lainie's laughter finally grew loud and disruptive enough to end the performance, she couldn't even tell what scene they were on. Priya was onstage, and then Alex, playing a campfire. Alex was wiggling and moving her arms and making a crazy sizzling noise.

"HA HA HA HA HA HA HA HA OH MY GOD . . ."

Brynn caught Tori's eye. She looked defeated. Not surprised, but defeated.

For a moment, they all just watched Lainie laugh.

It took a long time.

Finally, Lainie started gasping for air.

"Oh my god," she said, wiping tears from her eyes. "Oh, wow. I don't think I've laughed that hard in . . . my life."

Tori glanced at Alex, who had stopped sizzling. Alex's expression seemed to say what Tori was thinking: *This is not good.*

"It's unpolished," Sloan broke in insistently.

"That's right!" Candace agreed. "We're not wearing costumes, and we don't have any sets!"

"I'm not even wearing my belt!" Priya cried.

Sloan nodded. "Right now, it's just a big hunk of coal. But once we rehearse it and refine it and really make it shine, it'll sparkle like a diamond! You'll see."

"Oh, no, I won't." Lainie was already standing up and walking out to the aisle. "If I thought last night was a train wreck, I don't even know what this is. What's bigger than a train? A cruise ship?" She glanced at the stage. Tori and her bunkmates shrugged and nodded: Sure, a cruise ship was bigger than a train.

"It's like a cruise ship," Lainie went on, walking to the door, "ran into another cruise ship, pushing them into another cruise ship, and so on and so on, like dominoes." She paused and smiled. "It's like *twenty-seven* cruise ships piled on top of each other in a blazing, smoking mess of twisted metal. With all sorts of people bailing out in those little round life preservers. *That* is how bad this thing is."

Brynn gulped.

Lainie shook her head. "This protest is DOA," she announced. "You'd be better off doing nothing at all. If

102

I were a state congresswoman and I saw this musical, I would close the camp just to keep something like this from being written ever again." Now at the door, she wiggled her fingers in a tiny wave. "Ta," she said. "See you at dinner."

The door closed behind her.

Immediately Sloan turned to Brynn, already on damage control. "She's crazy," Sloan said. "You know that. She has no taste. We see what a great idea we have here. Sure, it's not perfect right now, but this musical has tons of potential!"

Brynn just shook her head dejectedly. "It's a cruise wreck," she said softly. "Lainie was right."

"She's *not* right!" Sloan insisted. "Come on, Brynn, believe! We can make this work."

Brynn shook her head again, looking from Sloan to the rest of her bunkmates. "Does anyone believe this can work?" she asked. "If even one of you believes this thing could convince state congresspeople to change their minds, speak up now."

Tori looked at her friends uncomfortably. Everyone seemed to be doing the same thing—looking from person to person, waiting to see if anyone was crazy enough to speak up.

Brynn sighed and looked at Tori. "See?" she asked.

Sloan frowned. "But if we don't do the musical, what will we do?" she asked. "How will we save Camp Lakeview?"

Everyone looked around at one another. Nobody seemed to have the answer.

"We don't," said Nat finally, looking close to tears. "We don't save it."

Everyone's face changed as they all slowly began to understand. They hadn't been able to think of a protest, so there would be no protest. Camp Lakeview would close as scheduled.

As the silence was growing, the dinner bell rang.

"Dinner," said Brynn, gathering her loose pages of script. "I don't know about you guys, but I don't have much of an appetite."

"I guess it's better to do nothing than to do something we don't believe in," Jenna was saying that night as a few girls stood in the bathroom, getting ready for bed.

It had been a solemn evening in bunk 6B. The musical idea had failed and nobody had a better idea for the protest, which meant that at their meeting with Dr. Steve the next day, nobody would have anything to say. They were all slowly coming to terms with the truth: no ideas, no protest, no chance of saving the camp.

Tori was unprepared for how miserable she felt. She knew she loved coming to Camp Lakeview; she knew she loved her friends here. Still, deep down, she had believed that even if camp closed, she would still see them in little get-togethers or hear from them via the camp blog. It wouldn't be the *end*. But now it did feel like the end of something. No matter what, they would never come together again in this space, sleep in these bunks, be surrounded by all of these people. For the first time,

Tori felt like she was understanding what it meant for the camp to close. Even if she went to surf camp next year, even if she saw all these girls again, it would never be the same.

Tori felt her eyes watering and reached up to wipe a tear away before everyone else could see.

Then, out of nowhere, she heard a loud *"No!"* Tori looked up. It was Jenna raising her voice. Across the bathroom, she was huddled with Nat, Alex, and Val, and Nat was speaking to the group in hushed tones.

"It *is* a good idea," Val said cautiously.

Jenna nodded. "Maybe. But this is getting ridiculous." She turned and looked right at Tori. "Why don't you just *ask* her, Nat? I'm tired of the tension between you guys."

Tori had no idea what was going on. "What are you guys talking about?"

Alex caught her eye. "What's going on is, Nat has an idea about how to save the protest."

Tori looked over at Nat. She was huddled down in her bathrobe, looking uncomfortable. But she met Tori's eye. "You do?" Tori asked.

Nat nodded. "It, um, it involves you."

Jenna turned back to Tori. "Nat needs to ask you if you'd be willing to do something, but she seems to think you're mad at her."

Tori laughed sharply. She couldn't help it. "I *am* mad at her," she admitted. "But last I checked, she was mad at me, too."

Val sighed, clearly tired of the conversation already. "Why don't you guys just make up already?

Look, we're all stressed about camp closing. But there's no reason we have to fight with each other about it."

Tori looked at Nat. She still didn't feel ready to make up. And judging from Nat's shell-shocked expression, her former best friend wasn't ready to apologize, either. "Why don't you just tell me what you want from me?" Tori asked.

"I have an idea about how to save Camp Lakeview," Nat replied, looking very serious. "But I need your help."

chapter
EIGHT

Tori looked skeptical. "What is it?" she asked. "And what can I do that nobody else can do?"

Nat took a deep breath. It was just as hard as she'd expected to ask her old (former?) friend for help. After their fight that morning, Nat had been sure they wouldn't speak to each other for days.

"Brynn's musical was kind of a mess altogether," Nat explained. "And to be fair, of course it was since she wrote it in a few hours. But there were moments in it that were good, right?"

Tori shrugged. "I guess."

"The thing is," Nat continued, "we don't have the expertise to make it work. But maybe— maybe if we got someone in here who really knows music . . ."

Tori raised an eyebrow. "Like who?" she asked. "I don't know anything about music. Do you?"

"No," Nat admitted, giving Tori a

meaningful look. "But I know who does . . ."

Tori looked behind her. Nat was looking out at their cubbies, right at Tori's care package from the other day, with the Judy Renaissance CD on top.

"Wait a minute, wait a minute," Tori warned. "If you're talking about Judy Renaissance, they're my *dad's clients*. I don't know them or anything. I can't just call them up and tell them we need them to save our little summer camp!"

Nat shrugged, still serious. "Can you try?" she asked. "They're from Harrisburg, right? And one of them even went to Camp Lakeview! Maybe it wouldn't be too much of an imposition. Maybe they would be into helping us out."

Tori took a breath. "I don't know," she admitted. "I've never done anything like that before. It's asking a huge favor of my dad—and I've never asked him to use his clients to get anything for me."

Nat nodded slowly. "Maybe it's time?"

Tori sighed. "This is going to be hard for me. I really have no idea how my dad will react. He might be mad at me for even asking. I mean, these are his *customers*, basically."

Nat was quiet for a moment. Finally she said, "Just now, when everyone was realizing that the protest is dead and we're going to have to deal with camp closing, how did you feel?"

Tori looked incredulous. "Are you kidding? I felt awful."

Nat nodded. "Me too," she said softly. "The question is, did you feel awful enough to take this little chance with your dad?"

▲ ▲ ▲

"Girls," Dr. Steve greeted Nat and her bunkmates as they all crowded into his office. "I have to say I've been looking forward to this meeting and seeing what you ladies have come up with."

Nat smiled. Brynn looked a little sheepish when she admitted, "Actually, it's kind of rough still. Kind of still at the outline stage. But we have some pieces of songs we can perform for you."

Dr. Steve looked a little surprised. "Um . . . all right," he replied. "Though I have to say, I thought you'd have a full presentation together by now."

Tori nodded. "We know, but we hit some roadblocks in the planning."

"These songs might be rough," Brynn added, "but they're full of heart."

"Yeah, try to think of them as works in process," Sloan agreed.

Dr. Steve nodded. "All right," he said slowly. "Shall we start, then?"

Nat stood up. "Just one moment," she replied. Quietly she walked out of Dr. Steve's office and then out of the building, into the bright sunlight of the sports field. There she met up with four "campers"—or at least, to the casual observer they'd look like campers. They were all crouched down to look shorter, decked out in Camp Lakeview T-shirts, sweatshirts, and baseball caps. Natalie walked them back into the building and through the door of Dr. Steve's office.

"Hello," Todd, the tallest "camper," greeted Dr. Steve cheerfully.

Dr. Steve looked confused. "Hello," he replied. "Am I missing something? Are there several extra people in this office right now?"

"Dr. Steve," Tori explained with a smile, "this is Judy Renaissance. They're a local band that I know of through my dad, and they've been nice enough to help us refine our protest."

Dr. Steve looked confused. "How on earth . . . ?" he began. "How did you get onto camp grounds with no one stopping you?"

Nat shrugged sheepishly. "I may have met them in the parking lot with some camp regalia."

Todd smiled. "I used to come here myself when I was a kid," he explained. "I don't remember you, though."

Dr. Steve nodded. "Before my time," Dr. Steve said. "Well, welcome, sirs, I suppose. I'm eager to see what you and these very creative ladies have come up with."

"Awesome," Billy, the guitar player, said. The band members looked around at one another and all hoisted their instruments in the air. Todd looked at Nat and her bunkmates.

"Ready, ladies?" he asked.

Nat nodded and smiled.

Billy struck an opening chord on his guitar, and soon the whole room was filled with bouncing, pulsing music. Nat couldn't help it—she bounced on her toes, swaying and shaking. It was *impossible* to listen to Judy

Renaissance's music and not dance. As the intro came to an end, she looked around at her bunkmates as they all opened their mouths to sing the first verse of the reworked "We Love Camp":

"Sitting on my bunk bed
Splashing in the lake
At Camp Lakeview, I feel a happiness
I don't have to fake."

As the chorus approached, Billy went off on an amazing guitar riff, and Frank, who hadn't been able to bring his whole drum set, began drumming wildly with his sticks on Dr. Steve's desk.

"We love camp!"

They were all dancing now, bouncing up and down and waving their arms to the beat. From where she stood, Nat thought they looked like a breathing, pulsing animal—all arms flailing, instruments wailing, and girls shouting to the beat.

"Save Camp Lakeview!"

Abruptly the guitars and keyboards stopped, and the band members took deep breaths and wiped their brows. The girls all fell back to earth, smoothing their hair and smiling at Dr. Steve.

"Wow," Dr. Steve said simply.

"It's rough," Nat rushed to explain. "I mean, the lyrics. We'll definitely refine them in the next few days before the protest . . . but we wanted to give you an idea of what the performance would be like."

"And the lyrics are all written by *us*," Brynn broke in. "Just so you know. The guys have helped us shape them up a little and adapt them to the music, but this is a pure camp-generated performance!"

Dr. Steve nodded slowly, looking from the girls to the band and back again. "And the . . . Judy Renaissance?"

Todd nodded.

"They're able to help you plan the protest and to be there on the day of?" Dr. Steve asked. "This isn't too much of an imposition on them?"

The band members shook their heads vigorously.

"Absolutely not," Todd replied. "Actually, we're between tours right now, so we're right in the area. And we're locals, dude. I came here as a kid. We know how much this camp means to the area, the kids that come here. If I knew there was some way that we could help and we didn't give it our all, I'd feel terrible!"

"And these are some incredible ladies you have here," Billy added. "*They* came to *us* with fantastic ideas—not the other way around. They're hard workers, too. It's been our pleasure to help them out."

Nat felt a warm feeling spreading through her insides. It was hard not to feel proud—both of herself for coming up with the idea and of her bunkmates for being so creative and smart with their contributions. For the first time, Nat felt like this protest might work.

Dr. Steve regarded them with a look of pleasant surprise. He kept looking from the girls to the band and back to the girls. Finally he cleared his throat.

"Okay."

The room was suddenly filled with shrieks, high fives, and peals of laughter. Natalie felt like her chest might explode, she was so relieved and excited at the same time.

"Is it okay if they come rehearse with us?" Nat asked. "I mean, not every day, but Todd said they could come the day before the protest."

Dr. Steve nodded. "That sounds fair," he agreed. "I'll leave a note at the camp entrance that these young men are our guests for the day."

"Omigod!" Priya cried, turning to hug Nat.

"Omigod!" Candace echoed. "We're actually *doing* this!"

Dr. Steve held up his hand. "Some ground rules," he went on. "You'll get the buses for four hours on Friday afternoon. Your counselors and CITs will go with you, as will I. You can spread the word to the other 6-level campers and CITs, and they can participate if they like. The younger kids will stay here."

Brynn nodded furiously. "Okay, that's all okay."

"And kids," Dr. Steve added, "I want to stress that I don't know anything that you don't. Your protest seems like it will be very fun and creative, but I don't know whether it will work. I want you to know that going in—this is a good effort, but it's no guarantee."

Sloan nodded. "We understand all that," she replied. "And of course if camp still closes, we'll take it as it comes. But I, for one, believe in our protest! Power to the people! The little people can change the minds of the big!"

Nat raised her fist in the air, along with several of her bunkmates. "Power to the people!" she shouted, then laughed.

Things were *definitely* looking up.

chapter
NINE

"Okay, guys!" Brynn shouted even though she was panting for breath. "That was awesome! Let's just try it one more time, same energy! Come on!"

Jenna sighed and tried to coax some energy back into her arms and legs. Her whole body felt like overcooked spaghetti, and she would have given just about anything to collapse into one of the chairs in the audience of the auditorium and take a three-hour nap. They'd been rehearsing the protest for two hours with the band, and they'd rehearsed on their own all day yesterday, rewriting their songs and changing the melodies to be bouncier and more upbeat. The rewrites seemed to be really working, and even Jenna had to admit that the last few songs had sounded *amazing*. But she was so tired.

Just then, a hand raised out of the sea of campers—lots of CITs and 6-level campers had taken the opportunity to join the protest—and a familiar, nasally voice cut through the din of low conversations.

"Brynn," Lainie called. "*Brynn*. Don't you think that last verse is a little awkward? If instead of, 'We'll get you with our mad rappelling skills,' we said, 'We'll get you with our mad *ropes course* skills,' then we could do a little pantomime, like we're climbing on the ropes course."

Lainie paused and did a little pantomime climbing, like she was the world's blondest spider. Jenna sighed.

"That's cute, Lainie," Brynn replied, "but I think I like it better the other way. Let's start again."

Todd and Billy glanced at each other, and the band launched into the song's intro.

"Hold on, hold on!" Lainie cried, waving her arms around. "Jeez! What does a girl need to do to get taken seriously around here? It's so hard to be an artist." She glanced down at Todd with a little conspiratorial smile, like he must understand what she meant.

Brynn set her mouth in a tight line. "What's the problem, Lainie?"

"The *problem*," Lainie replied, "is that I know you wrote these lyrics and whatever, but the simple fact is, my line is better." She looked around at the campers surrounding her and spread her arms in an *Am I right?* gesture. "Right? Who's with me?"

A dull murmur settled over the crowd as they started to argue—half for Lainie's change, half against.

"It's *definitely* better," a skinny redheaded boy named Jonah said, sending a lovelorn smile in Lainie's direction.

"Yeah," Kelsey, another CIT, piped up. "You

guys are all about power to the people, but who are the people? Don't we all get a say?"

Jenna sighed. The rehearsal had been going like this ever since Lainie had shown up for the first time this morning. "I heard your protest is worthy of my help now," she'd announced, and, just like that, flitted in and acted like she'd been right there and part of it the whole time. Lainie spent half her time trying to flirt with the band members—who, Jenna noted, all had serious girlfriends—and the other half coming up with ridiculous ways to "improve" the songs they'd been rehearsing for two days now.

Brynn looked livid. "It's not that big a deal," she insisted. "Can we just sing the lyric as is, like we've rehearsed it five hundred times?"

Lainie rolled her eyes. "*Ohhhh,*" she said. "I get it. We did it this way before, so it has to stay this way? There's no room for improvement in my brilliant creation?" She tossed her hair and looked thoughtful. "Actually," she went on, "is 'Campfire Bliss' even the right name for this song? What about 'Summer Love' or 'Kisses by the Campfire'?"

A murmur went through the crowd as everyone felt the need to discuss Lainie's suggestions. Brynn looked so angry, Jenna thought she could see steam coming out of her ears. This was bad. Lainie was derailing rehearsals in a big way. But what could stop her?

Suddenly Jenna had an idea.

"Actually," Jenna spoke up, and everyone startled, surprised to hear a voice from the back. "I don't think it was Brynn who came up with that lyric. I think it was . . . Todd, wasn't it?"

Todd looked at Jenna, surprised. Actually, the lyric was one hundred percent Brynn's, but Todd seemed just as frustrated as Jenna was about the constant back and forth with Lainie. More than once over the course of the afternoon he had begged, "Can't we just get on with it?"

Now Jenna caught his eye and gave a little nod—like, *Oh, yes, yes, it was.*

Todd started nodding, too. "Um, yes," he responded. "That was my lyric, yes, and I'm very attached to it."

Lainie looked stunned.

"Actually," Jenna continued, "I think Todd was saying earlier that's his favorite lyric in all the songs. And if someone changed it, he would probably, like, cry or something."

Todd looked a little taken aback now. He glanced at Jenna like, *Laying it on a little thick, are we?* But he said, "Yes, definitely. I would cry," and turned back to his guitar.

"Oh," Lainie said softly, looking a little sheepish. "Well, never mind, then. I would never want to upset you. You know what? Your lyric *is* way better." She pasted on a big, flashy smile. "Let's rehearse it again."

Just as Todd played the opening chord, though, the door opened and in walked a face Jenna hadn't seen for days: David. When she'd grabbed him at lunch the day before, he'd claimed he had just been "really busy" and hadn't had any free time to help with the protest the last couple days. But Jenna knew him better than anyone, and she knew he'd been avoiding her.

Jenna made a quick gesture to Brynn and hopped off the stage. *I'm going to take five*, she mouthed to her friend, who just nodded and turned back to the assembled chorus. Jenna kept walking down the aisle through the audience until she reached David, who looked like he wasn't sure how he felt to see her.

"Hey," she said softly.

"Hey," he echoed, looking from her face to his feet.

Jenna took a deep breath. "Listen," she said. "I said some things the other day that—"

David shrugged. "No, no, you don't have to apologize," he said. But he was still staring at the floor with an expression like someone had just run over his puppy. "If that's how you really feel."

Jenna paused, biting her lip. That was the thing, though, wasn't it? *If that's how you really feel?* More and more today, she was wondering about that.

"That's the thing," Jenna said, and was surprised to hear her voice crack a little. "I, um . . . I don't know if I really felt the way I said."

David looked up. "Huh?"

Jenna sighed. "I mean, when I said I didn't care about camp closing . . ." She trailed off and felt tears burning behind her eyes. "I guess in the last few days, I'm realizing I really *do* care," she said. "I mean, I always cared, I think. Maybe I was just trying to pretend I didn't to keep from feeling it. You know?"

David shook his head. "Um, no."

Jenna sighed again. "I mean, the thing is—now

that the protest is going well and really happening—I think that I really *care*." She paused. "I feel like we have a real shot, which is actually kind of scary. Because what if we don't? Then I'll get disappointed, you know?"

David looked at her carefully, nodding. "I guess."

"And that's the scariest thing I can think of," Jenna went on. "To think that I could believe it's all going to be okay and then suddenly have to deal with losing all of it—losing camp. Losing my friends. Losing"—and here her voice cracked again, and she felt a tear slip out —"*you* . . ."

"Hey, hey." David moved closer and then pulled Jenna into a hug. "You won't lose me. You'll never lose me. We'll still see each other." He paused. "You'll be fifty and thinking, like, 'When am I gonna get rid of this guy?' But I'll still be there."

Jenna had started sobbing, but she laughed then. "Okay. If you say so." She paused and pulled away. "It's going to be tough, though, Dave. If camp closes . . ."

"I know." David nodded. "I've been thinking about nothing else since Dr. Steve made his announcement. But we'll figure something out."

Jenna nodded, wiping tears away with the back of her hand. She leaned toward David and they hugged again. "I was never okay with losing you," she said quietly. "You know that, right?"

"I know." David squeezed her in a hug, then gently pulled away. "Now let's go! We have a protest to rehearse."

A few minutes later, everyone—even Brynn and the band members—was up onstage. Todd struck an opening chord, and Jenna felt herself start bouncing up and down in anticipation. They were rehearsing the final song of the protest, the rewritten "We Love Camp." With the help of Judy Renaissance, the campers had turned it into a bouncy, totally fun number, the kind of song you just couldn't stay still to. Todd had helped Brynn write some funny lyrics to the verses, which the campers all shouted to the beat as they bounced around. Singing this number was the most fun Jenna had had since the camp's closing had been announced.

"Bug juice by day
Prank wars by night
You don't have to tell me
I know this feels right."

Jenna and David bounced wildly, shouting the lyrics and dancing around each other. Jenna caught Nat's eye as she danced with Logan, and they shared a smile. All around her, Jenna's bunkmates were grooving, bouncing, having the time of their lives. Jenna smiled. It was the perfect end to the protest. Even if it didn't work and Camp Lakeview still closed, this was exactly how she wanted to remember her friends.

"We love camp!
We love camp!
Save Camp Lakeview!"

"That's a wrap!" Todd shouted.

chapter
TEN

"I can't believe we're really doing this." Sloan sported a grin from ear to ear as she and the rest of 6B lined up in front of Camp Lakeview's ancient green school bus. "I just can't believe the day is really here!"

Tori smiled. She had to admit, it was pretty exciting to *finally* be getting on the bus to Harrisburg. A little part of her had trouble believing it, too—that after all the bickering and the hard work and the struggle, they were really going to bring their protest to the state congress.

About thirty campers and CITs had joined the protest, enough to fill one bus. Dr. Steve was riding along with them, eager to see his campers in action. The members of Judy Renaissance were driving to the state capitol separately, and the plan was for everyone to meet them at the protest site right in front of the statehouse.

"Believe it," said Jenna. "This is *it*, guys. We have to give it everything we have because this is our big shot!"

The line was moving incredibly slowly, but

finally Tori and her bunkmates climbed onto the warm, musty bus. They walked down the aisle until they got to the last open rows, and then they started filing in. Tori watched as Nat slid into a seat and placed her faux Louis Vuitton purse on the other side. "I'm saving it for Logan," she told Jenna, who just shrugged and slid into the row across. *Of course*. Tori slid in next to Jenna, telling herself she wasn't even going to think about the Nat thing today. Today was all about energy and good vibes.

When everyone was finally seated, Dr. Steve stood at the front of the bus. "Are we ready, campers?" he asked, his arms spread wide and his face arranged in a crazy, eager grin.

"Ready!" Tori shouted, along with her thirty cohorts.

"Then let's *go*!" Dr. Steve gave the signal to the driver, who started up the bus—a noisy affair—and slowly turned around the circle drive and toward the camp exit.

As they drove through the narrow wooded streets that made up the area around Camp Lakeview, Tori felt herself relax. This was really happening. They were really about to try to save their camp, and it was partly because of her.

Tori leaned back and rested her eyes. The dappled sun coming through the trees and the rhythmic groan of the bus's ancient engine made her sleepy. Within a few short minutes, she had fallen into a dream, where she was on a car trip with her parents and driving through a weirdly familiar landscape. She looked down at the road and found that it was made of logs, like the cabins at

Camp Lakeview. Then she realized with a start that they were driving on the cabins. She tried to say something to her parents, but they had the radio turned up loud and couldn't hear her. Soon they were driving toward the lake, and Tori cringed as she realized that her father planned to drive right into the water! But just as they got to the lake's edge, a bridge appeared under them. Tori looked at the sign posted on the bridge's railing. HIGHWAY 101, it read. NEXT EXIT: FREE SWIM, ½ MILE.

"Guys, I want to get out!" she shouted at her parents. "I need to get out of this car! I want to be at camp!"

This time her mother turned around, a confused expression on her face. "What do you mean, Tori?" she asked, her brow furrowed. "There is no Camp Lakeview anymore. It's all over . . ."

"It's over," Jenna's voice broke into Tori's dream.

Tori blinked awake. They weren't on the peaceful country roads around Camp Lakeview anymore. Now they were on a huge interstate highway—or more specifically, on the side of a huge interstate highway.

The bus's engine let out a huge cough, rocking all of the campers. Then it made a sound like a sigh and fell silent.

"What?" Tori asked, rubbing her eyes and turning to Jenna. "What's going on?"

Jenna frowned, looking toward the front of the bus. "You missed it," she said. "As soon as we got on the highway, the bus started making these crazy coughing noises."

Tori blinked. "Okay. And?"

"And it sounded like it just gave out altogether," Jenna went on, her voice getting strained. "And that's bad because . . ."

Tori sat straight up in her seat. "How far are we from Harrisburg?" she asked.

"About half an hour," Gaby replied, turning around in the seat in front of them. "Close enough to taste it, too far to walk, basically."

Tori felt her stomach sink. "I'm sure the driver will be able to fix it," she said, trying to keep her enthusiasm up.

All around her, though, campers were exchanging worried glances. The celebratory vibe from earlier was gone, replaced by uncomfortable silence and nervous whispers.

"This can't be happening," Brynn wailed from the seat across the aisle. "After all the trouble we had just getting the protest together, the stupid *bus* breaks down?"

Tori glanced out the window, where the driver had disappeared under the bus. Cars were whizzing by them, making a *whoosh, whoosh, whoosh* sound. As she watched the cars going by, she wished she were in any one of them right then, happily on her way to her destination.

Dr. Steve, who had gone outside, said something to the driver and then climbed back onto the bus. "Kids," he announced, "we're having a little trouble with the engine. But Ed is doing everything within his power to try to fix it. For now, just sit tight."

He got off the bus again, and Tori checked her

watch. It was eleven twenty. The protest was supposed to start at noon, to coincide with the congresspeople's lunch hour. It would take half an hour to get there, which meant they had about . . . *ten minutes* to fix this and still be on time.

Thunk. Clang. Tori heard a muffled curse word as the driver, Ed, shifted under the bus.

This wasn't looking good.

▲ ▲ ▲

"What time is it?" Jenna turned over Tori's wrist, frowning deeply when she saw the time. "Wow. Um . . ."

"Yeah. It's not good," Tori said tensely. Around them, Brynn and Priya were deep into a game of rock, paper, scissors, and Nat and Logan were engaged in an increasingly violent tic-tac-toe tournament. Jenna had tried to interest Tori in a game, but Tori felt way too tense. She checked her watch every ten seconds. The driver, Ed, was still under the bus, and according to Dr. Steve's last update, there was no progress to report.

Tick tick tick tick tick tick tick tick. Tori felt like her watch was louder than a steel drum band. It taunted her with every second passing.

The protest had been supposed to start at twelve noon, and it was twelve twenty-seven.

And they were still half an hour away.

Tori glanced out the window and saw Dr. Steve say something to Ed, then sigh and wipe his forehead. He seemed to be asking Ed a question and not liking the answer. Tori watched as their camp leader shook his head, sighed, and started walking toward the bus door. She felt a trickle of dread in the pit of her stomach as he climbed the stairs and turned to face them all, looking defeated.

"Kids," he said gently. "I have some bad news."

"Nooooo!" several of the campers yelled back, shaking their heads furiously. They all knew what he was going to say. They'd been waiting to hear it for the last half hour. But that didn't make it any easier to hear.

"I don't think we're going to make it to our protest," Dr. Steve went on sadly.

Quiet fell over the crowd, quickly followed by some gasps and then a couple sobs. Tori looked over to see tears leaking from Brynn's eyes. She swiped at her eyes, frustrated, then sobbed and looked down at her lap.

"We *have* to make it," Sloan cried. "We've worked so hard! We can't let our voices go unheard because of some stupid *bus* engine."

Dr. Steve looked sympathetic, but Tori could see his mind was made up. "Believe me," he said to Sloan, "if I could think of any way to get thirty campers to Harrisburg in no time flat, I would do it. But we're stuck, kids. The bus isn't moving. We're going to have to call a tow truck and arrange for another bus to take us back to Camp Lakeview. It might be hours."

Tori felt tears wetting her eyes. This *had* to be the worst way to lose Camp Lakeview. To work so hard and come so close to saving it, only to be sent back at the last minute because of something they had no control over.

Dr. Steve looked around and found her in the

crowd, meeting her eyes. "Tori," he said, "I assume you have a phone number for the band?"

Tori nodded. "Yeah," she replied, and it came out like a sob.

Dr. Steve gave a sympathetic smile. "You'd better call them and let them know we won't be making it."

Tori nodded and let out a deep sigh, her chest shaking. She fished her cell phone out of her purse and scrolled down to Todd's number, trying to get a grip. *It's nothing worse than what we already feared*, she told herself. *Camp Lakeview will close. I'll go to Camp Ohana next year. Life will go on.*

But somehow none of that made her feel any better.

"Hey, Tori!" Todd's cheerful voice seemed totally out of sync with the scene on the bus. "Where *are* you guys, anyway? Stuck in traffic?"

Tori took a deep breath. "Not exactly." She paused, trying to keep from sobbing, but realized that she couldn't. Finally she just let it out in one big rush. "Our bus broke down we're still half an hour away nobody can make it go and we have to call a tow truck we can't get to Harrisburg and we're all so disappointed—"

"Wait a minute, wait a minute," Todd broke in. "Say what? You're missing the protest?"

Tori sniffled. "Yes."

"Because your *bus* broke down?"

Tori swallowed. Her throat felt hot and raw. "Yes," she said.

"Oh, no, we can't have that." Tori heard Todd

cover the phone with his hand and then muffled voices as he spoke to someone else. She wiped some tears from her cheek.

In a few minutes Todd was back on the line. "How many of you are there?" he asked.

Tori looked around the bus. "I'm not sure. Around thirty?"

The hand covering the phone again. And then muffled voices. Questioning voices, turning to excited voices. Then Todd's own excited voice, back on the line.

"Listen, Tori, don't any of you move a muscle. Stay right where you are. I have to make a few phone calls, but I think we can make this work."

Tori was confused. "But—"

"Shh. Stay put. I'll call you back in ten."

There was a *click* as Todd hung up the phone.

For a moment, Tori just held her phone in front of her and stared at it, like it might tell her exactly what Todd had up his sleeve. But soon, her bunkmates surrounded her.

"What happened?" asked Val.

"Yeah," said Candace. "Are they going home or what?"

Tori wasn't sure what to say. "He told us to stay put," she replied. "He'll call back in ten minutes."

The girls all looked at one another, confusion lingering in their eyes. Tori glanced out the window. Dr. Steve was outside again, talking on his cell phone and looking frustrated. Tori assumed he was trying to make arrangements to transport one elderly school bus and thirty extremely disappointed kids back to Camp Lakeview.

Tori stood up. "I don't know about you guys, but I could use some air," she said, heading toward the front of the bus.

Her bunkmates looked at one another. "Good idea!" Alyssa agreed. "Especially if we're going to be here for a few more hours."

Alyssa fell into step behind Tori, and soon most of the kids on the bus were filing down the aisle and into the bright sunlight. They all stayed far from the highway's edge, stretching and looking around at the woods that bordered the highway. Dr. Steve and poor Ed were on the other side of the bus, Ed still underneath, trying to figure out what was wrong.

"He wasn't mad?" Nat asked Tori, leaning back against Logan, who had his arms around her waist.

"No," said Tori. "I don't think so. He sounded disappointed, but . . ."

"Do you think they'll try the protest without us?" Chelsea asked.

Tori shrugged. "I don't know."

"Do you think they—"

Jenna's question was cut off by a loud beep from a small gray sedan as it shifted into the breakdown lane, slowed, and slid to a stop just a few feet from the bus.

Tori and her friends regarded one another: *What the . . . ?*

"Hey!" A slim, twentysomething brunette slid out of the driver's-side door and shouted to the assembly of campers. "Are you the kids from Camp Lakeview?"

Just then Tori's cell phone rang. Startled, she fumbled it to her ear and pressed talk. "Hello?"

"Hey." It was Todd's voice. "I arranged for some friends of mine to carpool you guys to the protest site. It may take a little while, but just sit tight, and eventually I'll have enough rides for all of you. Okay?"

"O—" Tori stopped. "Wait a minute! There are thirty of us!"

Tori could hear the smile in Todd's voice as he replied, "I have a lot of friends."

Tori laughed. She couldn't believe he was being so nice. "But—but—"

"But nothing!" insisted Todd. "Get your energized butts into the cars and get down here! We have a protest to make!"

"But—it was supposed to be at noon!" Tori's heart was beating fast. She loved the idea that they might be able to save the protest, but—wasn't it too late? Hadn't they already missed the lunch hour?

"Noon, schmoon!" Todd cried. "We've got tons of daylight left! Just get in the cars."

Even in her shaky state, Tori knew that she'd have to run that one by Dr. Steve. "You should talk to our camp director," she told Todd, walking around to the other side of the bus and holding her cell phone up to Dr. Steve, who seemed to be between his own phone calls. "Someone needs to speak with you."

As Dr. Steve took the phone, Tori walked back to her friends.

"What's going on?!" cried Brynn.

"Yeah," said Sloan. "Did Todd arrange some way

for us to get to the protest?"

Tori nodded, still not quite believing it. "They sent their friends," she said, waving to the lady by the gray sedan. "They want to give us all rides to the protest and go through with it. Can you believe it?"

Joy seemed to spread through all of the assembled campers. Suddenly the air was filled with laughter and high fives. "Omigod," Priya gasped, a huge smile on her face. "Omigod! We still have a chance! We can save Camp Lakeview!"

"We missed our protest time," Tori pointed out, voicing the one reservation she had left. "It won't be the lunch hour. There won't be as many people around."

Jenna rolled her eyes. "Tori! So *what*?" she asked, smiling encouragingly. "Don't you think the songs we rehearsed are exciting enough to draw them out of their offices? Don't you?"

Tori thought for a second, then laughed. "Yeah, I guess so."

Jenna beamed. "So we're back in business!" she cried.

Just then, Dr. Steve was walking around the bus with Tori's cell phone in his hand and a confused expression on his face. "That was Todd," he told Tori.

"I know," Tori replied, suddenly nervous. Would Dr. Steve let them get into cars with people he didn't know? Would the protest be killed by him?

"He had an unusual request," Dr. Steve went on.

Tori nodded seriously. "I know," she said.

Dr. Steve nodded gravely, stroking his chin in thought. "So three of you had better get going," he said, gesturing to the gray sedan, where the driver was still waiting with a smile on her face.

It took Tori a second to figure out that he'd said yes. But when she did, before she could think about it, she threw herself at him in a hug. "Oh my god, thank you!" she cried. "Thank you! Thank you! I'll go!"

She pulled away and looked at her friends.

"Me too," said Brynn.

"Me three!" cried Sloan.

Together they ran over to the gray car and introduced themselves to the driver, whose name was Tessa.

"Thank you so much, Tessa," Sloan said as they settled into the car, buckling their seat belts.

"Any friend of Todd's is a friend of mine," Tessa replied. "We went to high school together, and I know his causes are very important to him."

"This is the most important cause of all," Brynn told her. "Saving Camp Lakeview!"

Tessa smiled, turning the key in the ignition and putting the car in gear. "Then let's get to it, shall we?"

chapter ELEVEN

An hour later, all of the campers stood together on a small green across from the statehouse. The members of Judy Renaissance bustled around, making last-minute adjustments to their instruments and arranging themselves around the crowd. Nat felt her heart beating a million miles an hour. This was *it*. The protest was about to start. This was their last chance to save their camp.

Todd faced the group of campers, his guitar resting on his hip. He looked to Brynn, who stood in the middle, their unofficial leader.

"Are we ready to rock Harrisburg?" Todd asked.

Brynn broke into a huge smile. "Ready!" she cried.

"Then let's get started!"

Todd played the opening chord of the first song Brynn had written, "Lakeview Pride." Nat felt her heart beating in time with the music. All of the campers began bouncing nervously, getting ready for their first line. And then it was time, and thirty voices rose together to belt out the lyrics:

"You say you want to close Camp Lakeview
I don't think you know what that means
My heart resides in its old cabins
My soul rests in the auditorium's beams."

Instantly the whole area was filled with music, and passersby paused to take in the spectacle of thirty teenagers and three grown men dancing around and belting out these bouncy songs. Nat sang her heart out, swaying with the music, snuggling with Logan, and dancing with her bunkmates when the music picked up. Soon they were all dancing like goofballs, showing off all kinds of crazy moves and laughing almost as much as they were singing. Nat couldn't remember the last time she had had so much fun. It was probably, she figured, the way she used to feel about lots of things at camp before Dr. Steve had announced it was closing and she had forgotten what fun was.

"Up next!" Brynn shouted when the first song was over. "A song I cowrote with my friend Sloan, called 'Power to the People'! It's about the citizens' right to make their voices heard! And that's just what we're doing!"

Todd began the song, and Nat sang forcefully about something she had come to believe in: making her voice heard. *Maybe*, she thought as they all sang together, *maybe this protest won't work. Maybe the state congress won't change their mind. But at least we can know we did something—we used our voices.*

And people seemed to be listening. Lots of people were stopping to take the pamphlets Sloan had made up explaining the Camp Lakeview story, and many of them also signed the petition she'd quickly thrown together. When the second song ended, a tall redhead paused in front of the group.

"Hey!" she said. "I went to Camp Lakeview for three years when I was a little younger than you kids! I didn't know it was closing."

Sloan nodded. "The state congress wants to use the land to build a highway."

The woman bit her lip. "Wow! What a waste of that beautiful spot!" She shook her head. "Well, I signed your petition. I hope you stop them!"

"Thanks!"

As the woman walked away, Brynn turned around and smiled. Nat smiled back.

"I'm so glad we're doing this," Brynn said. "I'm so glad we're at least *trying*."

Jenna smiled. "Me too."

"Me too!" cried Tori.

"Me too!" chorused Nat and a bunch of the other campers.

"Are we ready for the next song?" Todd asked, and when the campers affirmed that they were, music filled the air again. The girls all got really into the music, dancing and making crazy faces as they belted out the song. Pretty soon people who stopped to watch were dancing along, sometimes even singing the chorus with the campers. The whole green had turned into a party.

One song blended into the other, and even when Nat's feet were sore from dancing and her throat was sore from singing, they all kept going, still as into the songs as they had been when the protest started. Soon their petition was filled with signatures and the green was filled with sympathetic bystanders who sang along with their songs and pumped their fists in time to the music. It was getting late, and they had all been through their whole program of songs and had started again at the beginning. Two more songs and Nat knew they'd probably have to pack it up.

Suddenly a petite, well-dressed woman appeared on the green, watching them with an amused, impressed expression. She waited until their song ended, then stepped forward.

"What was the title of that song?" the woman asked.

Brynn smiled. "It's called 'Power to the People,'" she explained. "It's about how important it is for citizens to speak up about issues that are important to them—like us, speaking up about how Camp Lakeview can't close!"

"Yeah!" called Sloan, and several other campers hooted their agreement.

"Well, that's very impressive." The woman smiled, exposing perfect white teeth. "Maybe I should introduce myself. Ladies and gentlemen, I'm State Representative Tanya Bierden."

Nat felt her jaw drop. She looked around at her bunkmates: *Wow.* This was *her*—the woman responsible for the decision to save Camp Lakeview!

Sloan looked just as surprised as Nat felt. "Wow," she said. "Did you—I mean did we—have you changed your mind about closing the camp?"

The woman smiled again, and her expression was warm. "I'm afraid I can't commit to anything right now," she said. "But I just wanted to tell you how pleased I am that you've come today and, like you said, made your voices heard. It's the citizen's job to tell us what's important to him or her! I wish more people your age believed in their power as strongly as you do."

Sloan grinned. Most of the campers smiled proudly.

"Thank you for coming out to tell us that," Brynn said quietly.

"You're more than welcome," Representative Bierden said. "I would love to shake all of your hands, if you'd grant me the privilege."

The campers all looked at one another and silently formed a line to shake hands with Representative Bierden. When it was Nat's turn, she smiled proudly. She had never been involved in any sort of protest before—it had never even occurred to her that she *could* protest something. But she had to admit, it felt great to speak out.

"Thanks again, ladies and gentlemen," Representative Bierden said when she was done. "If it is at all possible to save your camp, I promise to look into it. I hope you all enjoy the days you have left and have safe travels home." She smiled again and then turned and walked back to the statehouse.

"Wow," breathed Sloan.

"Wow," agreed Dr. Steve, who had been standing off to the side during the protest but now stood before them, smiling proudly. "Campers, I think we've accomplished what we set out to do. Now we should head back where we belong—back to Camp Lakeview."

Alex made a face. "But wait—how will we get home?" she asked. "The people who drove us here live around Harrisburg. They're not going to want to drive us two hours away."

Dr. Steve just grinned, gesturing behind him. "Ladies and gentlemen, I give you—your *bus*!"

Nat looked past Dr. Steve, and sure enough, there it was—she wondered how long it had been parked there! The ancient Camp Lakeview bus idled at the curb, with their trusty driver and handyman, Ed, waiting in the doorway.

"Ed kept fiddling with it and was able to find the problem about half an hour after you all left! The bus is running well now and, Ed promises us, has plenty of power to get us home. So let's load on!"

Nat looked at her friends and smiled, pausing to take one last look at the green and burn these last few hours into her memory. The protest had been everything she loved about camp—hanging out with her friends, just having fun and expressing themselves. She wanted to remember it forever—especially if it was going to be one of her last camp memories.

After a few seconds, Nat followed her friends and got back on the bus. They were headed back to Camp Lakeview. Back home.

On the bus, Nat watched as Logan settled into their old row, smiling and patting the space next to him.

But a few rows behind him, Nat saw Tori, smiling ear to ear with her face flushed, looking like she'd just had as good a time as Nat had.

Nat paused by Logan's seat. "Logan," she said, "I'm going to sit with Tori for a sec, okay?"

Logan shrugged and smiled warmly. "Okay. See you in a few."

Nat reached over and squeezed his shoulder, then walked back to Tori's row.

"Is it okay if I sit here for a second?" she asked Jenna, who was facing backward, kneeling on the seat and talking to Alex, who was sitting behind them.

"Sure." Jenna slid out of the bench and went to sit next to Alex. Nat met Tori's eyes, feeling weirdly nervous. But why? She and Tori had been best friends for years now. They'd only been fighting for a week or so. So why did it feel like Nat couldn't even remember what it was like to have a normal conversation with Tori?

"Hey," Nat said hesitantly.

Tori looked blank for a second, like she wasn't sure yet how to respond. Then she nodded. "Hey," she said back, just as hesitant.

Nat slid onto the bench beside her friend. "Listen, I know things have been weird between us lately."

Tori nodded. "You can say that again."

Nat sighed. "I just . . ." She paused. "I don't want to fight with you, Tori. You're one of my favorite people in the world. I know I've probably been a little weird these last few weeks, with the news of camp closing and knowing that Logan and I might have to break up.

I just wanted to say, whatever I did that made you mad, I'm sorry."

Tori looked touched. "It's not just you, Nat," she said softly. "I guess my feelings were hurt when you didn't jump at the chance to go to Camp Ohana with me. I didn't get why you wouldn't choose me over Camp Lakeview. But when we found out camp might be closing, I started to understand why you weren't all excited to leave. I get it now. I hope you know that."

Nat nodded. She felt a tear leaking from the corner of her eye. "I do."

Tori sighed. "The truth is, I can't even figure out why I've been mad at you. Maybe I don't have a good reason. I was a little upset you were spending so much of your free time with Logan, but even that's not it."

Nat smiled weakly. "I'm sorry about that. I know I haven't been hanging out as much lately. It's just . . ." She swallowed.

Tori smiled sympathetically. "You're really into him," she said.

"Yeah." Nat nodded and let out a little laugh. "I really am. And we might break up, and I don't know what I'll do."

Nat stared into her lap. Suddenly she felt Tori's arm around her shoulders, and then Tori gave her shoulder a little comforting squeeze.

"I'm sorry, Nat," Tori said softly. "Whatever happens, you'll always have me. I'll help you through it."

Relief flooded through Nat. It was funny, she'd almost forgotten what it felt like to have a close friend who had your back. It was so great to have Tori in her life again—to know that whatever boys came or went or broke your heart, your friends would always be there.

"Maybe that's it," Tori continued, softly. "Maybe in a weird way, we've been trying to prepare ourselves to lose each other. You know, with camp closing. Maybe we're trying to get ready for the hurt by moving away from each other. You know?"

Nat sniffled. "That's, like, the stupidest thing to do in the world," she said. "We only have another week together!"

"It may be stupid, but I think we were doing it." Tori squeezed Nat's shoulder again.

"Tori," Nat said, turning to face her friend, "I'm so sorry. Let's go back to normal for this last week, okay?"

"Okay."

Nat leaned in and hugged her friend tight. "And we'll still see each other, even if camp ends," she went on. "Right?"

"Right!"

They hugged again, and Nat swiped some tears from her eyes with the back of her hand. "Thanks," she said softly.

Tori nodded. "Have you—um—talked to Logan about it?" she asked.

Nat sighed and shook her head. "I haven't been able to get the words out," she admitted. "But I think it's time."

▲ ▲ ▲

Nat slid back into her seat with Logan and tried to smile. "Hey," she said.

"Hey," said Logan, reaching out to take her hand and squeeze it. "Feel better?"

"Much."

Logan nodded. "This has been such an amazing day, right?"

Nat nodded and swallowed. "I hope it works."

Logan's expression softened. "Me too." He squeezed her hand again and then looked out the window.

"Logan . . ." Nat had to push the words out; every fiber of her heart was telling her not to say them. "What . . . what . . ." Her voice cracked.

Logan turned back to her, concerned. "What's up, Nat?"

Nat blinked and swallowed, trying to push down the fear she felt. She *had* to ask him. She had to know.

"What's going to happen to us if Camp Lakeview closes?"

Logan sighed. A darkness fell over his face, as though he'd been hoping to avoid the subject, too. "I don't know, Nat," he said honestly. "You know I'm crazy about you, right?" He squeezed her hand once more.

"Right," Nat said softly, trying not to let her voice break.

Logan sighed again. "But we tried the long-distance thing last year, and it was so hard." He paused. "And Nat, we're only fourteen. Maybe we're too young to be tied down to someone who lives so far away."

Nat felt a sharp pain in her chest, like someone had stabbed her, and then the pain was gone. She felt tears burning behind her eyes but blinked a few times, trying to keep them inside. She took a deep breath and then another.

"So we'll break up," she said, and her voice was strained, but she didn't cry.

Logan closed his eyes. She could see he was hurting, too. "Maybe," he said, and then rushed to add, "but we don't know what's going to happen, Nat. Camp Lakeview might stay open. Maybe we'll see each other next year and be ready for something more serious. You never know."

Nat squeezed his hand back and nodded. "You never know," she agreed softly.

She sat quietly for another minute, breathing slowly, in and out, waiting for the heavy feeling to lift from her chest. It amazed her to realize that she felt all right. Definitely not great, but not like she wanted to curl up in a ball and drown herself in tears, either. Maybe she'd been expecting this all along—deep down, she'd known this was what he'd say. Because it made sense. And as much as it hurt . . . she knew he was right.

Logan was still watching her with a concerned look. She sighed, and he wrapped his arm around her, pulling her close so she could rest her head on his shoulder. He looked down at her, his eyes warm, and she gave him a small, sad smile.

"You okay?" he asked.

"I will be," she replied. "I think we're all going to be fine."

EPILOGUE

August 25, 2007

To the outstanding campers of Camp Lakeview,

It is with great regret that I inform you that after much consideration, I have come to the conclusion that it is necessary to close the doors of your beloved camp.

I am, as you know, a representative of the citizens of Pennsylvania, and I simply wouldn't be doing my duty to them if I allowed the proposed state highway to be built on a different piece of land. I've spent hours staring at maps, manipulating them, trying to figure out a way to both get my citizens this much-needed highway and save the camp that you so enthusiastically defended in your protest. I'm afraid it's just impossible. I must uphold my vote to claim Camp Lakeview's land.

I wanted to write to you, however, to let you know that your protest did touch me, and I hope that your enthusiasm for "making your voices heard" will never fade.

I am sorry that we couldn't come to a different conclusion. And I hope that your many beloved memories of Camp Lakeview will bring you smiles for years to come.

Sincerely,

State Representative Tanya Bierden

"We can't stay here forever." Alex stood by the edge of the lake, watching her friends and looking back toward the cabins nervously. "The buses are going to leave . . ."

"In half an hour," Jenna finished for her. She stood stock-still, feeling the breeze on her shoulders as she stared out over the crystal blue lake. All of the girls of 6B had embarked on a "memory hike" to say good-bye to the grounds—walking from place to place, talking about the good times they'd had in each one. In her mind, she could hear the shouts of her friends at free swim, their squeals of victory when they won a race or finished a long, tough swim. She was remembering endless games of Marco Polo, lazy afternoons suntanning on the bank, and flirting with David on the raft out in the middle of the lake.

"We have to say a proper good-bye," Nat agreed. She swiped an impatient hand over her eyes, which were still wet from her big good-bye with Logan. They'd decided to break up, like she'd half expected. And it hurt. Already she was wondering what he was doing without her, if he was missing her as much as she missed him. She knew this was the right thing, and she knew she'd be okay eventually, but still—it wasn't going to be easy.

"I can't believe this is the last time I'll stand here," Val murmured, kicking the sole of her flip-flop across the sandy beach. "I thought I would come to Camp Lakeview every summer until . . . until I got too old and they kicked me out!"

Priya laughed. "I think a lot of us felt that way, Val," she said.

"Guys." Alyssa checked her watch and glanced back to the cabins. "I hate to cut our hike short, but we *do* need to get back if we want to act on . . . on the secret plan."

Tori smiled. Alyssa had shared her "secret plan" for leaving their mark on Camp Lakeview a few days before, and Alyssa's mom had overnighted the necessary materials. None of them were eager to stop their lazy, memory-filled final hike around the grounds, but Alyssa was right: It was time to get going.

"Okay," Tori agreed. "This is tough, guys, but let's pack it in."

They all took one final look at the lake. Tori closed her eyes and imagined herself floating in an inner tube, daydreaming with all her friends surrounding her. Trying to keep the image in her brain as long as possible, she finally opened her eyes and saw most of her friends starting to head back. Reluctantly, she fell into step behind them.

Back at the cabin, Becky and Dahlia were busy taking inventory of the furniture inside and making sure that none of the campers had left anything. Alyssa ran over to her duffel bag, unzipped it halfway, and pulled out a brown paper sack. "Hey, Becky," she called. "We're going to go hang out on the green for a few minutes, okay?"

"Okay." Becky's head appeared in the doorway. She looked out of breath. "Say your good-byes, kids, but don't get too sad. You know you'll all stay in touch! And you all have my address."

Alyssa smiled. "We'll try not to."

Following Alyssa, they all walked over to the green clearing in front of the mess hall. It was where they'd held most of the all-camp activities, like games. Jenna sighed, remembering all the good times she'd had there—the gossip, the giggles, the crazy conversations. She wondered what she would be doing next summer. Hopefully, it would involve David.

"Okay." Alyssa held the paper bag in front of her and pulled out a small packet. "We'll start with Sloan. Sloan, I picked a sunflower to represent you because it seemed earthy, enthusiastic, and warm, like you. It always seems to be smiling, and you do, too. So here are your seeds."

Sloan came forward and took the little packet from Alyssa. "Thanks, Lyss." She paused, then gently ripped the packet open and sprinkled a few seeds into her palm. "Guys, I know I'm the newbie and that I've only been coming to camp one year, but I've learned so much from all of you. I'm so glad I got to know you and that I had at least one year at Camp Lakeview before it closed. I'll always remember our protest. That was an amazing day in my life."

Alyssa pulled a small spade out of the bag, and

Sloan crouched down, opened a hole in the ground, and carefully planted a few sunflower seeds. Then she stood up.

Alyssa pulled another packet of seeds out of the bag. "Candace, for you I picked a violet. Because it's really beautiful, even though it does kind of blend into its surroundings."

Candace smiled. "It blends into its surroundings?"

Alyssa laughed. "Well, maybe it *mimics* its surroundings."

Candace tilted her head. Everyone knew she had a habit of repeating everything everyone said. "Mimics its surroundings?" she asked, then came forward and took the packet from Alyssa. Tearing it open, she said, "Guys, I know I'm not as talkative as some of you, but I love coming to camp. I've loved getting to know you guys. And I'm so glad I'll still get to hang out with Brynn, at least, and keep in touch with you guys on the blog."

She carefully planted a few violet seeds next to Sloan's sunflowers.

Alyssa pulled out another packet. "Val, for you I picked a marigold. It's steady, it's loyal, it's bright, and it's beautiful."

Val smiled and came forward, taking the seeds. "Thanks, Alyssa," she said. "I can't even tell you guys how much I'll miss you. I've loved getting to know you all and seeing you change through the years. We've had so many crazy times together. Remember all the Color Wars?"

Everyone laughed, remembering the crazy competitions.

Val crouched down and carefully planted her

marigolds. Then it was Brynn's turn.

"Brynn, for you I chose a dahlia," Alyssa explained. "Because it's bold, colorful, and dramatic."

Brynn came forward and took the packet. "Thanks, Alyssa," she said. "Guys, I don't even know where to start. I've always loved to pretend, but you guys taught me how to be real, how to have better friends than I even imagined, and how to trust myself." She swallowed. "I'll always remember acting in the camp shows and seeing you guys all in the front row, clapping like crazy. So thank you for that."

She knelt and planted her seeds.

Alyssa pulled out another packet. "For you, Gaby, I chose a miniature rose," she said. "Because it's beautiful and it smells really sweet, if you can get past the thorns."

Gaby faked shock. "Are you saying I have a thorny personality?"

Alyssa looked sheepish. "Um," she said. "Maybe a *little* thorny? But sweet underneath."

Gaby shook her head. "I told you, I'm a much nicer person than I used to be."

Alyssa smiled. "Actually, that's true. But I've known you all along, so you get the thorns."

Gaby just laughed and took the packet. She turned around, about to speak, and tears formed in her eyes. "Guys . . ." she said. "Guys, I know I haven't always been the *easiest* person to get along with. When I came to camp, I was a little bossy, and then I lied to you guys about my brother . . ." She paused. "I just wanted to say, though, that you guys are the best friends I've ever had.

Honestly. You've always been there for me, even when I was less than perfect to you." She swallowed. "I'll miss you guys so much. So thank you."

She knelt and planted the miniature rose seeds.

Alyssa pulled the next packet of seeds out of the bag. "For Jenna," she said, "I chose daisies. They thrive in any location, and they're fun and don't take themselves too seriously."

Jenna stepped forward. "Oh, you *guys*," she said with a delighted smile. "Seriously, I . . . I don't even know what to say. I feel like Camp Lakeview is a *part* of me. I've never had as much fun in my life as I've had here. All those prank wars, competing in sports, getting to know David . . . I don't know what I'm going to do without this place." She paused and wiped a tear from her eye, looking as surprised as anyone that she was actually crying. "Like, thinking about next summer, I just . . ." She stopped herself before she started all-out sobbing. "I love you guys," she finished quickly. "And I'll miss you like crazy."

Jenna planted her seeds and stepped back into the crowd, enveloped by hugs. Alyssa pulled out the next seed packet.

"Priya," she said, "for you, I chose the sweet pea. Because it's bright and playful."

Priya came forward, smiling. "Thanks," she said, taking the seeds and kneeling down. "You guys, I've had so much fun here over the past three summers. When I first came, I thought I would just have a blast hanging out with Jordan. But then I met all of you, and I realized what fun really is. All the hanging out, sharing secrets, crushing on boys—I really love you guys. We *have* to stay in touch. Promise!"

"Promise," echoed a few of the girls as Priya planted her seeds.

"Tori," Alyssa went on, pulling out another seed packet, "I brought you hyacinth. They're glamorous and they smell really sweet. You've been so great about keeping us up to date on the latest trends, sharing all of your dad's inside secrets with us."

"Thanks." Tori smiled and took the packet. "You guys, I'm so glad I met all of you. When I came to camp the first time, I thought I'd hate it. Sleeping in a cabin and sharing a bathroom with nine other girls? No thanks. But you guys made this place feel like home. Now I can't imagine what I'll do with*out* Camp Lakeview." She looked at Nat. "I've made some of the best friends of my life here," she said softly, her voice breaking. "I'll miss you so much."

Tears spilling over, Tori knelt down and planted the hyacinth bulbs. As she stood up and Nat enveloped her in a hug, Alyssa continued.

"Chelsea," she said. "I got you snapdragons because they're bright and feisty and have a quick mouth."

Chelsea made a face as she came forward to collect her seeds. "Thanks," she said, and then helplessly broke into a smile. "You guys, I know sometimes my mouth gets me in trouble. I haven't always been the easiest person to get along with. Sometimes I said things I shouldn't have. Okay, I did that a *lot*." She grinned ruefully. "But these summers—they've been incredible to me. The best times of my life. You guys are all amazing—some of the coolest people I've ever known. And I don't know what I'm going to do without you."

Wiping a tear from her eye, Chelsea knelt down and planted her flowers. Alyssa reached into her bag and pulled out the next batch of bulbs.

"Alex," Alyssa said, "for you, I chose tulips. They're strong, elegant, and colorful. You're such a great athlete and so dependable."

Alex came forward and took her bulbs. "Thanks, guys," she said, looking embarrassed. "I can still remember when I first came here. It seems like decades ago, not just years. I remember being worried that you guys would be weird about my diabetes, like that even mattered. You guys are the best friends I've ever had. I'll really miss this place."

She knelt and planted her bulbs, and Alyssa went on.

"For Nat," she said with a smile, "I chose the iris. They're sophisticated and unexpected, just like you."

Nat felt tears leaking out as she came forward and took the bulbs. "Alyssa," she said, "you're the first friend I made at camp. I remember when I first arrived, I couldn't believe I was even here. Just like Tori, I thought I would *hate* Camp Lakeview. I was afraid of your reactions when I told you about my dad and scared of living in the country all summer." She smiled. "Now I can't imagine what my life would be like if I'd never come here. If I'd never met you guys. I just—I'm so glad I met all of you."

She knelt and planted her flowers.

Alyssa pulled the last packet from the bag. "For myself, I chose the hydrangea," she said, pulling out a bulb. "They're cool and kind of dreamy. Just like me." She smiled, kneeling down to plant her flowers. "Guys, you all mean the world to me. Even when we're fighting, you're all so smart and feisty and awesome. You open me up and pull me outside myself. And I'll always be grateful for that."

She shoveled a little dirt over her bulbs and stood. "I guess that's it."

"We'll always be here," said Priya.

"That's right," Jenna agreed. "Even if they build the highway just a few feet away, our flowers will live here forever. Together. Just like they belong."

Nat gulped and felt tears coming again. Just then they heard the grinding of the Camp Lakeview buses pulling to a halt in the parking lot. Stunned, they all faced one another.

"I guess this is it," Chelsea said. "The beginning of good-bye."

They walked back over to the parking lot. All of them were teary, and occasionally a sob would escape one of their mouths. The counselors were helping load luggage into the buses, and campers were crowded everywhere, saying one last good-bye.

Dr. Steve stood in the parking lot, holding a bullhorn. "Campers!" he announced, and his voice boomed over the whole grounds. "Campers, we're going to start loading up the buses now. I just wanted to say—" His voice broke. "It has been my privilege to host you at this camp and be part of this time in your lives. Camp Lakeview may be closing, but it will live on in your memories for the rest of your lives. And I have been lucky enough to know you all, and I will remember you forever. Good luck, kids."

Nat felt tears streaming down her face.

"Time to load up bus number one!" a driver called. "Bus number one! If you're on bus number one, please move to the front!"

Nat and her friends all looked at one another.

"I'm on bus number one," Jenna admitted.

"Me too," said Gaby.

"Me three," added Alex.

Another driver began yelling to the crowd. "Bus number five!" he called. "We're loading up bus number five!"

"That's me," whispered Alyssa.

"And me," added Brynn.

"And me," Candace said sadly.

The girls were all standing in a circle, staring at one another. It was like nobody wanted to be the first to say it. But finally Alex did.

"I guess this is good-bye."

Nat felt herself exploding into tears. And her tears set off everyone else, so soon they were all sobbing, shaking their heads, hugging one another. Nat felt like her body was trying to turn inside out. She couldn't remember the last time she cried this hard—so hard, it hurt.

"Good-bye, guys," said Jenna.

"Good-bye," whispered Alyssa.

"Good-bye, my best friends," said Alex.

"Good-bye, my best summers," added Gaby.

"Good-bye, lazy afternoons," said Priya.

"Good-bye, midnight gossip sessions," said Tori.

"Good-bye, working together," said Sloan.

"Good-bye, Color Wars," laughed Val.

"Good-bye, flirting with boys," said Chelsea.

"Good-bye, campfire secrets," Candace added.

"Good-bye, Camp Lakeview," Nat finished. They all moved together in a huge group hug and squeezed one another tight. When they finally let go, all the bus drivers were yelling.

"Bus number two!"

"Bus number four!"

"Bus six!"

Silently, wiping tears away, the girls all quietly made their way toward their separate buses. Nat was the only person from 6B on bus four. It was going to be a long, lonely ride home. Taking one last look at this place that felt so much like home, she climbed aboard.

As more kids piled on and the bus started up, she stared out the window at the place where she'd done so much growing up. When she'd first come to camp, she couldn't believe she was setting foot on Camp Lakeview, or any camp grounds at all, for that matter.

Now she couldn't believe she was leaving.

The next spring came late, and the ground was saturated from the snow. What used to be Camp Lakeview was quiet, except for the sounds of construction over where the mess hall used to be. All of the structures had been torn down, and only the raft in the lake remained, floating lazily in the sun.

In the middle of the green, though, a few hesitant sprouts emerged. They grew and grew and finally erupted into blossoms. Sometimes the construction workers would walk by and wonder who had decided to plant such pretty flowers in the middle of the wilderness.

The flowers themselves were strong and hardy. They filled the green with color and thrived on Camp Lakeview's land. Together. They spent the summer, and every summer thereafter, swaying lazily in the breeze, frozen in time.